...and Nobody Knows it but Me

By Megan Stockton

Printed in the United States of America

First Printing, 2023

ISBN 979-8-9854017-2-1

Any references to historical events, real people, or real places are used fictitiously.

Cover design by Dagan Boyd
Editing by Dagan Boyd

Printed and produced using KDP, an Amazon Platform.

Bad Luck Cat Publishing
Grimsley, TN
https://www.meganstocktonbooks.com

Dedication

This one is for my editor, Dagan, who has been here for me through so much. She is an amazing human and does not realize how much she means to me. Thank you for making sure my books are tidy and making me keep going even when I feel like I can't.

i.

It had been a brutal winter that year. The wind had grown teeth and the world seemed to have lost color, warmth, and light. Swathed in a bath of blue coolness, curtains closed, door locked, hearth cold. She had once told him how she felt like it had never been this dark before, and how the days seemed to grow shorter but somehow lasted forever. She couldn't stand how long the days felt, how long she had to go between sleeps. It was the only way she seemed to be at peace: when she was sleeping. But she didn't sleep much those days.

He had heard her pacing around the cabin more than once, feet shuffling across the wooden floor in a rhythmic pattern, humming old songs to herself. She would walk from one end to the other, pausing only long enough to look from one resting place to the next. She would sometimes cry, but if he would call her name, she hushed immediately and insisted she was 'okay' before the pacing began again.

It was like she haunted him then, even before she truly did.

one

At fifteen minutes until six, it was already growing dim outside. The sun seemed to rupture around the seams as it hit the horizon, spilling gold across the aegean haze. Shadow stretched its deep purple fingers across the pelt of snow on the ground, broken up only by the mountainous landscape. It reminded him of home. The only place that had ever felt like home. While the winters here were mild and fleeting, he was accustomed to places where all anyone knew was the cold. Anytime he felt the coolness of the year's twilight, he felt like he was there again.

Lakin Douglas was struggling against the hypnosis that he felt as he watched the fluffy snow fly towards his windshield like stars at hyperspeed. The wipers went from stiff arms to flapping back and forth to warped soft lines across his windshield. The drive had been exhausting. He had the option to stop somewhere halfway, and he had really considered it. He hated to waste the money on lodging just to rest his head and decided to move on and drive through the night. Now he felt the effects of that decision, even with his passenger side floorboard steadily accumulating empty energy-drink cans.

It was cold inside the vehicle, not much warmer than outside. Lakin had always driven like this when it was cold. He didn't turn on his heat, unless he needed to defrost his windows, and he bundled up. It made exiting the car less of a shock, kept him from getting sweaty under his layers, and also kept him awake.

He passed a sign on the right that read 'Rotten Fork' but had no other information about the town he was entering. Just a single long plank of wood with the town name and zip code. Simple, but somewhat foreboding.

Rotten Fork.

He had taken it upon himself to research the town name on the way here because of its peculiarity. He discovered that Rotten Fork was named for the tributary it was situated on, an offshoot of the larger Gray River. Rotten Fork was small and curved back into its mother river, but in the extreme bend where the land was most fertile, it also stagnated into a swamp. Apparently that still blackwater carried a unique odor. It wasn't uncommon for tannic, sulfuric, iron-rich waters to have this stench. The charming town name, however... that was unique.

A little town appeared around him, not much more than a straight line between an alley of buildings, like one of those old west movies. A few buildings stretched on either side of the central four way, but otherwise there was not much to speak of. A few cars slowly drove through the snow, yellow lights illuminating the disappearing asphalt.

Lakin pulled his car up to the courthouse, where he saw the jail was also located. The parking spaces were all empty. He trudged out of the car, slipping slightly on the slick sidewalk as he approached the front door. It was locked. He turned around, shrugging his oversized coat up around his ears, breathing through clenched teeth until his gums were cold and dry.

An SUV pulled into the parking space behind him, and a man casually exited the vehicle, making his way up the stairs to where Lakin stood.

"Mr. Douglas?"

The man who approached was dressed in a police bomber jacket with a silver star embroidered on his jacket and the word 'Sheriff' above. He was tall with a thick beard and equally thick hair that curled out from beneath the beanie on his head. His nose was narrow and slightly crooked.

"Sheriff Lowell?" Lakin asked quietly, reaching forward to put out a hand.

"That's me. Call me Shaw, please. Welcome to Rotten Fork."

"It's a nice little town,"

"Been through many like this I'm sure, but this is ours," Shaw said with a smile. "I'd invite you inside, but unfortunately they closed the sheriff's office here years ago. No funding."

"So are you..." Lakin motioned to his jacket.

"Yeah, yeah. I'm with the county now. Station's in Last Bend."

"So can you tell me a little bit more about what's going on here?"

Lakin had once been regarded as one of the best at dealing with problem animals. Of course, he often carried the opinion that the animals were rarely the true problem. Sometimes when humans' and animals' habitats overlapped... there was conflict. Unfortunately, the people had the dollar.

"We think we've got a rogue wolf or a pack, maybe... killing livestock, causing some issues. If there's a way to deter them or something the farmers can do to help keep them at bay... well, we'd like to know."

Lakin tried to pretend he was listening intently, nodding as he crossed his arms over his chest. When Shaw had finished, he spoke, almost a little too quickly. "There haven't been wolves in this part of the country since the thirties, Mr. Lowell. Now, that being said... there still may be a nuisance animal, but there's a good probability it is a roaming domestic dog or something similar."

"This was no dog, Mr. Douglas. No disrespect." He laughed, patting him on the chest. "You're the expert. There are still wolves in Rotten Fork."

Lakin didn't argue, he just nodded. Sometimes it was easier not to fight with people. Everyone thought they saw a mountain lion on their game camera when, given their geographic location, it was more likely to be a chupacabra. Sometimes it was easier to gather the evidence and then tell them you told them so when you could actually prove it.

"I'll have to look at some of the carcasses of the animals, any prints or scat. See if we can identify a species or subspecies, patterns, and then track them."

"We don't have much in the way of tracks or anything for you to look at right now, I'm afraid."

Lakin blinked, forcing a smile. "Well, it'll be hard for me to figure anything out if I don't have more than witness accounts to go on."

Shaw laughed, waving his hands back and forth at chest level as he snarked, "Well, it took you three weeks to get out here. We can't really leave rotting animals lying around and put tents over pawprints while you pussyfoot around."

Lakin swallowed back a retort. "My wife passed away a month ago, that's four weeks ago. Twenty-eight days, actually."

Shaw's demeanor changed immediately, the sarcasm and sass melting away to genuine sympathy. "Mr. Douglas..."

Lakin didn't give him time to continue, instead committing to what he was saying. He set his jaw. "Your request came in eighteen days ago. The facility delivered me the request four days after that. I wasn't even sure I was ready to go back to work at all, but here I am." He somehow regretted saying all of that, making Shaw feel like shit. Lakin had too much empathy to be an asshole like this, even when it was deserved.

"I understand," Shaw said quietly, dark eyes shifting away. "As... as frequently as the attacks have been, I'm sure there will be another. In the meantime, I do have some trail cam footage from a local that I'm trying to get exported and also some photographs. I can deliver those to you in the morning if you want to get settled in tonight."

"Great." He had expected more of an apology, more regret. "Where's the closest hotel?"

"No hotel in Rotten Fork."

"Bed and breakfast? Rental? I was told there would be somewhere for me to stay."

He felt a fleeting pang of concern that he would be put up with someone who lived nearby. The last thing he wanted right now was to have to stay with someone. He just wanted to be alone with a nice bed and maybe some good coffee for the morning.

"No, but I have a hunting lodge just outside of town you can stay in, free of charge, if you're okay kind of roughing it while you're here."

Lakin nodded again, relieved. "Yeah. I'm more comfortable roughing it anyway."

"A man after my own heart. If you wanna follow me out there, I'll get you a key and make sure the power is on. Come on, your eyebrows are freezing."

Shaw made descending the icy stairs look easy, skipping down them much faster than he had walked up. Lakin took his time, careful to step on the large chunks of salt that were still visible. The sheriff's vehicle rumbled to life, groaning and growling as it shifted gears and sailed out of the parking space and onto the road. Lakin was more cautious. He had noticed the roads were poorly maintained here, especially for the weather. Without proper scraping and salting, they would be impassable in a few hours. He knew that was another downside to the small town life: just no funding for this type of maintenance.

He was less tired now, reinvigorated by the conversation with someone living. The ice on his windshield caused his wipers to make a dry and dragging sound, like her feet rustling across the floor every night.

two

The Lowell hunting cabin was a modest building with very few frills; four walls, a floor, and roof. Lakin was impressed as he entered, however, leaning his hands against the wood of the interior. It was made of good wood, really good wood. Not one of those do-it-yourself log cabin kits you buy online. This wood was mostly hardwood, slow-grown and old. It had maybe even been harvested locally: trees that had stood there for ages and ages and become resistant to mold, decay, and insects. It was a good cabin of good construct.

It reminded him of the one that he and his wife had shared, the one that he'd built with the help of some local boys with carpentry skills. It had been beautiful, homey, warm, and dark. It had smelled sweetly of moss and lacquer. Sometimes he felt like it was alive, moaning slightly with pressure changes and developing petrichor after every rain. It was a place now that he only visited in his nightmares, where it was sometimes still bedecked in flame against the night sky.

"She's not much," Shaw said, leading Lakin inside. The way he smiled when he turned around to face him suggested that he was proud of this building, despite the way he brushed it off as nothing special. "But she'll be a comfortable place to stay, nice and cozy."

He flipped on the light switch, satisfied when the bulbs all came on to offer a soft yellow glow. With confirmation that the power in the cabin was working, he flipped the lights off again. Lakin noted that it was fairly warm in the cabin, and there was a decent amount of stove-lengths stacked by the fireplace. There was a very modern stove, somewhat out of place in the otherwise rustic cabin, the head of a white deer with asymmetrical antlers above the mantle, and a stuffed bobcat perched below.

"There's nothing here to eat, but there's a couple of places in town. The roads are going to get bad tonight, but I think it's been warm enough that they'll melt off by midmorning. I could run and get you something for dinner and bring it back if you'd like?"

Lakin shook his head. "Nah, I'm not hungry. I'll be fine for the night. Thank you, though."

Shaw shook his head, wringing his hands together. "Listen, I'm really sorry about your wife. I had no idea you'd lost her so recently."

"Of course not," Lakin said quietly. "How could you?"

"Well, it was insensitive of me to not consider your personal schedule and affairs in the first place.. I hope I'll be able to make it up to you somehow before you head out."

"Don't worry about it."

Lakin offered his hand as a gesture of good faith, and Shaw shook it enthusiastically. The sheriff headed out the door and said with a smile, "I think we're going to get along great, Douglas."

As the door shut Lakin muttered, "I doubt that."

He stared around the quiet cabin for a few moments, taking off his shoes and placing them beside the door. Until he got a fire going, he left his socks on, a hole in the heel giving him a hint at the chill on the floor. The cabin had an isolated warmth that seemed to just barely stave off the cold.

Lakin threw his two bags onto the bed and then brought his laptop inside. He unpacked his clothes and folded them neatly onto the trunk at the foot of the bed. He turned on the laptop and set up his hotspot. He already had a file ready for this investigation. His theory remained the same for now: domestic dogs. The feral dog could cause serious damage and was a very real liability. They would get into a group and, with that pack mentality and 'peer pressure,' they were often violent. They would do things the individual dogs of the group would never do on their own: kill other animals, maul children, attack adults.

His stomach growled, and he folded his arm against it. He hadn't taken the time to eat anything other than a pack of peanuts from one of the half-dozen gas stations where he'd stopped to either take a piss or refill on whatever energy drink had the angriest-looking mascot on the front. Tomorrow he'd wander into town and find a good little mom-and-pop diner and order their daily special. He loved those types of places.

Lakin started a fire, stoking embers until they turned into long tongues of flame. Warmth emanated, and he pulled off his socks and laid them to warm overnight. The scents of amber and birch began filling the room as he removed the quilt from the bed and also placed it in close proximity to the hearth. Nothing like a warm, heavy blanket to help him sleep.

There was a rapping on the door, a gentle knocking that he barely heard. He initially wondered if he had heard it at all, pausing only long enough to look at the darkening wooden door, wind howling outside of the windows. The knock came again, and he stood hesitantly, moving over to crack it open and peer through the crack into the white-and-blue night.

A woman stood outside, bundled up with most of her face covered by thick scarves. She wore a pink toboggan with a little fluff on top. She held a big blue bag in her hands, laid across her forearms like a pizza delivery man. Her mouth was covered, but he could see her smile with her eyes, pink cheeks rising up underneath the sparkling blue irises.

"Mr. Douglas?" her muffled voice came from beneath the layers of fabric.

"Yes, ma'am," he responded with a polite smile.

"My name is Marie Baldwin. My husband and I live just down the road, we're friends of Sheriff Lowell's, and he mentioned to us that you'd be up here... looking into the wolves. I brought you something to eat, if I can come in?"

He opened the door to allow her inside. She stomped her brown boots off outside, snow flying off in chunks before she came inside. She immediately dethawed, leaving puddles of water wherever she went. She seemed to know the layout of the cabin already, laying her bag on the table and opening it up to reveal a still-warm glass baking dish full of some sort of cheesy casserole. Lakin thanked his lucky stars that this woman somehow read his mind and brought him something to eat.

She took off her hood and scarf, leaving the toboggan on her head and down over her ears. Her nose and cheeks were pink from the cold, and she sniffled.

He sat down and allowed her to serve him. "Thank you, Mrs. Baldwin."

"It's my pleasure. I'll have a bite with you, if you don't mind."

"Not at all. What do you know about the animal attacks?" Lakin asked, taking one of her plastic forks and plunging it into a piece of the casserole to examine it. He detected shredded chicken, mushrooms, and broccoli. It was a little dry but flavorful and filling. He tore apart larger chunks of chicken with his tongue against the roof of his mouth as she talked.

"Plenty, I guess," Marie said, picking at her casserole more than she ate it. He wondered if she was hungry or just lonely. "One of our son's heifers was killed a week or so ago. I don't think we were the first to lose something to them, but it was us that told Shaw about it first. It was... just unusual. She was in a paddock, not out in the field. Whatever it was got in, killed her, just cut her into ribbons. Didn't eat no part of her that we could tell. Tony thought that maybe someone killed her because they were jealous... My son shows the cows."

"Tony?"

"He's my husband," she remarked quietly, laying her fork down. "Other people have had issues, though. Pets, livestock, you know. Shaw says it's only a matter of time before they get brave enough to attack a person."

"If it's a wolf, that could be true," he agreed.

"You don't think it's a wolf?"

"I don't know yet."

She looked at him for several moments, and when he looked back at her, he thought he could see the dark-pink circles under her eyes grow in intensity. She looked down, shrugging. "What else do you think it could be then?

Lakin expected that he would have to deliver this theory a dozen times or more during his stay, at this rate.

"Dogs... that's my best guess right now. The most likely perpetrators."

"You mean like... dogs? Labradors or something? Would they be capable of killing a cow like that?"

"You would be surprised what a small group of dogs is capable of. They get together, goad each other on. They're just whirlwinds of destruction."

Marie looked down at her plate, scooting it off to the side. She pulled her fraying toboggan down on her head. "I better be going before Tony comes looking for me. Welcome to Rotten Fork, Mr. Douglas."

Lakin nodded at her, standing to offer his hand. She clasped it in her now gloved one, pink and fingerless mitten curling into his larger palm.

"Thank you for dinner, Mrs. Baldwin. It was delicious."

She smiled at him, waving awkwardly just at the height of her waist before retreating back into the cold night.

three

Lakin wasn't sure what had helped him fall into such a deep slumber, but he was thankful for it. He heard the knocking at the door in his dreams first, and then he slowly pulled himself into awareness. His head felt heavy and full of delirium, like he had something stiff to drink the night before. Chills ran through him as he tried to stretch the sleepiness from his limbs. Whoever was at the door kept knocking a rhythmic pattern: one, two-three, one, two-three.

It was early enough that the light outside was still hazy. He shuffled across the room to half-heartedly throw on a bathrobe, pulling it closed sloppily in the front as he cracked the door open, squinting into the pale light with one eye.

"Sheriff Lowell."

"Please," the man said, removing his hat with a smile. "Remember? Call me Shaw."

"Shaw. What can I... what's up?"

"Well, I'm sorry to have woken you up on your first night's sleep…"

Shaw pushed his way inside, despite Lakin's reluctance to let him in. He pulled the robe around himself even closer. He didn't like the way that Shaw seemed to look him up and down, like he was sizing him up, like he was somehow threatened by him.

Shaw continued, chipper, "Oh, did you use the stove? How'd she do for you?"

Lakin blinked. "No… I didn't use the stove."

"Oh… just noticed the plates. Thought you'd cooked yourself some dinner. Which is fine… This place is yours while you're here."

He nodded. "Oh, that. A lady stopped by after you left last night and brought me a casserole. A miss…"

"Let me guess… Marie Baldwin?"

"Yeah, that was it."

"Doesn't surprise me that she'd be up here snooping around." Shaw bit his lower lip, putting his hands on his hips and shaking his head. "Gotta watch women like her."

Lakin started to ask him what he meant by that, because he had found Mrs. Baldwin to be innocent enough, but he didn't want to encourage Shaw to talk to him any longer than he had to.

"Anyway," Shaw went on. "Another wolf attack, just like I promised you. It's not too far down the road, if you want to ride out there with me and see what you think."

"Yeah... I can do that. I'll just throw some clothes on if you'll give me a few minutes."

"Oh, yeah, sure. No big deal. I'll just be out in the truck."

Lakin lingered in the center of the room for several moments after Shaw exited, waiting until he heard the truck door shut outside before he started getting dressed. He pulled on his warm, long socks and then the rest of his clothes. He loaded the batteries and SD card into his camera and hung it around his neck before tucking a small notebook, pen, and caliper into his coat pocket.

He took the time to walk into the bathroom, which he had not visited since he had come here the night before. He checked his hair in the mirror, the mess untamable but easily hidden by a head covering until he had time and peace to take a shower.

Shaw was sitting dutifully in the truck, visible through the swipe of the wiper blades as they scattered small tufts of snow that attached themselves to the glass.

The truck was toasty inside, a little too warm. He could feel heat blowing against his feet, like his toes were on fire. He pulled them against the seat as closely as he could to avoid as much of the uncomfortable warmth as possible.

"Where do they live?" Lakin asked, buckling his safety belt across his lap and laying the camera atop the chest strap. He wasn't sure how long he could handle the heat, reaching over to rest his finger on top of the window button.

"Just down the road, actually... should take us less than five minutes."

"What happened?"

"Something got a goat. Seems like it could be our mystery animal."

Lakin nodded, staring out the side window. He didn't want to be here and regretted taking this job so soon. He should have given himself more time, but part of him had craved some kind of human interaction. Before she died, he had always loved being alone;taking a day trip by himself to fish and camp by the stream, going to get a cup of coffee and read a book in his car with the music playing softly. He had always cherished solitude. When she was gone, the moment she was gone, solitude became loneliness. There was a sudden, vast emptiness. A strange new type of quiet. Even when he tried to pretend she wasn't gone, just away, he could sense her absence. She was truly gone, even though his heart held out the smallest hope that this was just a bad dream. It was still surreal.

Sometimes, he couldn't tell what it felt like to be awake anymore. Not what it had felt like before, anyway.

He had gone back to work at the lab because he wanted his old friends around him, those people who had known him before he had been married, before he'd even met her. They knew what he was like before, and it soothed him to know that there was a before. That he wasn't entirely reliant on her existence. He did so feel like he was withering away... They would tell him that he looked good, patting him on the back, but their eyes wouldn't stay on his face. They'd look somewhere between them, fingers squeezing his shoulder. Let us know if we can do anything for you. Anything at all. He didn't want them to say that, to offer that. He had once done the same, and someone had taken his offer. It had changed everything. It was why he was in this place.

The vehicle jarred him as it bounced across a gravel driveway. He imagined that in the warmer months the passage was even rougher, without the packed snow and ice to make things just a little smoother. A little farmhouse loomed in the distance, one that he imagined had been built decades ago. It had a slight sway to the roof, an overall shift and tilt towards the sunshine.

An old truck that couldn't have been much younger than the house was parked in the driveway: red paint chipped with orange rust, duct tape wrapped around the driver's side door handle. A man stood in the yard, pacing as he talked on a cell phone. He wore only a winter coat and his boxers, a pair of boots extending nearly to the base of his knee caps. The snow had already begun to melt in the sunny parts of the yard, creating a wet slush. Lakin exited the truck before Shaw had even unbuckled, taking a deep breath of the cold air.

Shaw walked over to the man in the yard as he put his cell phone away. They shook hands, and Lakin slowly headed towards them. He could see Shaw motioning for him to hurry, but Lakin continued to take his time just to spite him.

"This is Mr. Douglas," Shaw said. "He's with the Wildlife Lab in Obey."

The man standing there was too thin. His frame was large, but it was like he didn't have the meat to cover it. His cheekbones and jaw were sharp, with skin stretched not tight enough over everything, sagging in all of the crevasses. His eyes were liquid: wet and without much form, sunken into his skull.

"Mr. Douglas," the man repeated. "Thank you for coming out here."

Lakin took the man's frail hand, shaking it gently. He could feel the bones in his wrist and fingers grinding and cracking. He was afraid the entire limb might just snap off in his hand.

"It's my pleasure, Mr..."

"Simms."

"Mr. Simms. Can you show me where you lost your animal?"

Simms nodded, leading the two men back past the leaning house and out to the pasture that lay beyond the barnlot. There, in what was left of the snow, lay a mutilated goat. The snow around him was painted purple with blood, like an oversaturated snowcone. The snow had started to melt with the warmth of bodily fluids, making a larger pool around it in the mud.

Lakin didn't know much about goats, but he supposed this had once looked like a pretty nice goat. It had a dappled coat and neatly trimmed hooves. He couldn't see where an animal had fed on the goat, but the body looked like it had been shredded with knives. Pieces of flesh bulged from beneath the spotted coat, and guts peeked out from multiple gaps in the body cavity. The head was entirely gone, missing at the end of the thick neck. It wasn't a body part he imagined an animal would carry away.

He took photos of the body, especially of the wounds.

"Do you have a dog, Mr. Simms?"

"Did... She went missing night before."

"Kind of cold to come out here barefoot, wasn't it?"

"I got boots on, Mr. Douglas."

Lakin smiled at him, pointing at the ground around the goat. "Prints don't lie."

Simms and Shaw both approached, looking at the soft ground that peeked through the melting snow. Lakin had noted the barefoot human footprints. He was a little annoyed, as they had muddled the animal prints that were also there.

"Looks like a big dog was here too,"

"She was an Anatolian Shepherd."

"Could've been her."

"She don't go nowhere, Mr. Douglas. She's gone, I haven't seen her since the night before last. Something's got her."

"Are you sure you weren't out here barefoot, Mr. Simms?"

"That's a little ridiculous," Shaw interjected.

"No, I came out in my boots to feed everything. That's when I found the goat."

"What time do you think that was?"

Shaw spoke again, "Why would he be out here barefoot?"

"I'm just trying to determine if there's another possibility here."

"What possibility?" Shaw asked.

"Maybe it isn't an animal at all."

Shaw laughed, "Are you going to ask him if he had an insurance policy on the goat next?"

"No..." Lakin breathed, flustered. "No, that's not where I was going with..."

Simms looked back and forth between the two of them. "Are you suggesting I killed my own goat?"

Lakin opened his mouth, trying to speak through his discomposure. Shaw waved his hand in the air, speaking instead, "No, no. I'm sure Mr. Douglas doesn't mean anything by that."

"I just want to know if anyone in the house was out here," Lakin snapped. "Someone, somebody was out here."

Simms grumbled, "No one was out here. I live by myself."

Lakin squatted down, pointing at the ground. "Do you see this, Mr. Simms? Sheriff Lowell? It's a clear footprint, an adult's."

"All I see is a dead boer," Shaw said, shrugging.

"If I wanted someone to spout bullshit, I would've called... I would've..." Simms stammered, trying to come up with something clever. He spat, spinning around and walking back to the house.

Shaw looked over at Lakin. "You've got to work on your people skills."

"What are you talking about? I was trying to ask him questions about this. Someone was out here. You were the one agging it on."

"Well, it sounded accusatory," Shaw insisted.

"Okay," Lakin muttered, stepping over the animal's body as he tromped through the soggy field.

"Where are you going?"

"Following the footprints while I can still see them."

"I don't think Mr. Simms would want you running around the property. Not after that interaction."

Lakin didn't respond or acknowledge him, following the footprints as they went from indentions in the mud to dirty tracks in the snow. His own feet ached just thinking about running around without shoes in weather like this.

"He'll probably be back with a gun," Shaw called after him.

Lakin continued on, even after he heard the sheriff say he'd be waiting in the truck. The tracks led to the tree line, where skeletons of oak, sorrel, poplar, and ash stretched into the sky.

four

Lakin had driven himself to the small grocery store on the northern end of town later that evening. He was getting a craving for snacks, and the small cabin had nothing pre-stocked in the cabinets. He pushed the buggy through the bright white store, noting the chemical aroma and general absence of life. The luminescence of the lights made it look all the more dark outside the large windows.

The produce and meats looked fresh, high quality. Small towns like this always had some of the highest quality goods, but people would rather have the convenience and low prices of a big box store. It was a shame, really. This part of the world was dying off, slowly, hanging on by its rotting teeth.

Someone ran into his buggy with theirs, shoving the handle back against his hips and knocking him backwards. He regained his footing to avoid falling, but not before he knocked a few cans of pink salmon onto the floor with his elbow.

He turned to the woman who had collided with him, smiling apologetically as though it had been his fault.

"So sorry," he said, bending down to catch a rolling can before it disappeared under the shelving forever.

The woman rushed to help him, crouching down on the floor to gather the cans in her arms. Her pale face flushed pink with embarrassment, straw-blonde hair tucked behind her ears and spilling down her back. She stood up and deposited the cans into his buggy.

"No, it was my fault, I'm sorry. I was just... somewhere else," she insisted, picking at a button on her vest nervously.

He laughed, "I don't think I need that much salmon."

"Oh, right..."

They started putting them back onto the shelf together, and she spoke again, "Not a fan of it, then? Always liked salmon patties myself."

"I never could cook them. My wife can make the best salmon patties. She puts cream cheese..." he suddenly paused, taken aback by his sudden enthusiasm... and catching himself speaking in the wrong tense. He closed his slack jaw, patting a can against his opposite hand before he put it back onto the shelf.

The woman cleared her throat. "Are you new around here? Haven't seen you before."

"I'm just visiting. Lakin Douglas," he quickly offered a hand, swallowing the dry lump that lodged itself in his throat, just at the back of his mouth.

Her eyes suddenly lit up, and she grasped his hand with both of hers, squeezing. "Mr. Douglas. I'm Mrs. Lowell. My husband has told me so much about you."

He was surprised, somehow, that this woman would be married to Shaw Lowell. It wasn't that Shaw was an unattractive man: rugged, gruff, hairy almost as an animal would be. Some women were into that. It also wasn't that Mrs. Lowell was unattractive; quite the opposite, actually. She was somewhat plain, the type of woman that you thought you had a chance with. She glowed with animation, blue eyes glistening with genuinity. Maybe he had Shaw all wrong. She certainly had him questioning his evaluation. She was girl-next-door, but there was something in her eyes along with the purity. Something that suggested some sublime deviancy.

"I'm sorry about your wife," she went on. "That must have been so hard. I can't even imagine what you've been through. Was she... was she sick?"

He cleared his throat, "Yeah."

It was more complicated than that. She had a disease that no one could cure, although he often told himself that if he'd been paying attention, if he had noticed, if he had loved her enough... he could have helped her. Healed her from that dark cancer that had started in that spotless soul of hers. The heart that made her cry when the dog died in the movie, that made her take a piece of paper and a cup to catch and release every spider that invaded their home. She had never had any hate in her, no ill will. How was it that something so dark crept in? Where did it come from? Why her? Why her?

"Well, Shaw can be a little pushy, so I'm sure he's already told you, but if you need anything while you're here, don't hesitate to let us know. We really appreciate you coming out here to help everyone, especially so soon after such a terrible event."

"I thought you two lived in Last Bend." Lakin attempted to drive the conversation somewhere else.

"Oh, no. We live right here in the Fork."

The Fork. That was a nicer alternative to Rotten Fork, he thought.

"The police station is there, since the city lost funding for their own station. Shaw drives up, it isn't too far. His family has always lived here, for generations. I think they were some of the first people to settle down in this area. Anyway, I'll let you get back to your shopping. It was good to meet you though."

"Yeah, you too."

She pushed her buggy past his, and for a moment he stood there staring down at the empty basket. When he turned around and stole a look back at her, she was looking too.

five

He woke up in a cold sweat, breath escaping his lungs as though he had been forced to run for miles. His chest was on fire, tight like a rag being rung dry. He put his palm over his sternum, fingertips detecting his fluttering heart. He conveniently could not remember his dream, as so often happened. Maybe some sort of preservational instinct locked the horror away from his consciousness, shielding him from the trauma in the real world. Don't look, please don't look.

He slipped his feet onto the rug beside the bed, briefly burying his toes in the long fibers. The cabin was so quiet that he could hear the faint ringing inside his skull. He got up and started a fire, stacking the wood in a precise manner before starting the flame. Warmth immediately pooled around the hearth.

Coffee was necessary, but the pot was full of cobwebs from disuse. He brought it to the sink, stream of water running, and prepared to rinse out the interior. A long-legged cellar spider was poised inside, papery-thin body bouncing on his breath as he peered inside at her. She was barely a thing, but still. He took his hand, cupping it to fit inside, and he scooped her and the web out and deposited it into one of the north corners of the wall. She kicked the web free from her legs, repositioning herself on the mess of her home, but she would rebuild.

Satisfied, he rinsed the pot and started a brew. He had found an off-brand medium roast with hazelnut, his favorite flavor. The aroma filled the cabin as it gurgled and sputtered, slowly filling the pot. While it brewed, he took a quick shower and changed into clothes suitable for the outdoors. He planned on walking the property around the cabin, with Shaw's permission, and some of the local public land to search for signs of predators.

As he poured himself a mug of the warm coffee, he heard his phone ping from the bedside table. He walked over slowly, observing the lit screen as it displayed five-or-so green messages and missed calls across the front. He was notably bad for not paying attention to his phone, leaving it on silent most of the time. He didn't recognize the number that had called three times, or the text message that read mr. douglas pls return my call at ur earliest convenience. thx.

He noticed that Shaw had also given him a call, the most recent missed caller on the list. He took a long sip of the coffee and inhaled, dreading the call already. He didn't know what it was about that man, but their personalities obviously just did not mesh.

Lakin reluctantly dialed Shaw on the phone, setting his blue-speckled tin mug on the table as he collapsed into one of the creaking wooden chairs.

"Lakin," Shaw said, voice as bubbly and enthusiastic as usual.

"Yeah, I saw you'd called. Sorry, I was in the shower."

"Have enough water?"

"Yeah. I wasn't in there long."

"If you notice low pressure or if the water shuts off completely you may have to walk out to the spring house and thaw the pump out. We have a guy named Ivan who usually does that for us, but since you're staying for a bit, I didn't want him wandering around disturbing you... so it's just down the trail behind the cabin. Kind of steep, but a pretty straight shot to the springhouse."

Lakin hummed an 'uh-huh' in his throat. "What did you need today, Mr. Lowell?"

It seemed like every time Shaw talked, he forgot why he started a conversation in the first place. He never quite cut to the chase.

"Claire said she saw you at Fresh Mart last night."

Lakin paused before responding, taking the time to deduce that Claire was likely Mrs. Lowell. He wondered what she might have said about him.

"Yeah, I bumped into her."

He laughed, but the sound was cold. "She said she bumped into you."

Lakin shifted uncomfortably. "So has there been another animal attack or any new information?"

"Oh, yeah. Nearly forgot... I know a guy named Chitto who does a lot of hunting, asked him if he'd talk to you about some of the tracks he's seen out. He took some photos."

Lakin imagined blurry pictures that you could barely decipher, Bigfoot quality prints in the dirt. Someone else who had already made his mind up about what he'd seen and what he expected.

"Yeah, where can I find this guy?"

"I'll text you his number. Talk to you later."

"Alright."

He didn't wait for the text as he called the mystery number on his phone, the one that had left him a plethora of messages and missed calls. A man answered almost immediately.

"Ye-hello."

"Hey, this is Lakin Douglas, I saw I had a message and a few missed calls from this number. May I ask who I'm speaking with?"

"Oh. Oh, Mr. Douglas." The man sounded far away for a moment, like he'd swapped ears and kept talking. "This is Owen Mayer. Shaw told me you were in town to help out with some of the odd stuff going on and, boy, have I got something you need to look at."

"Okay, Mr. Mayer..."

"Owen, please."

Lakin wondered what it was with these people insisting he use their first names when they'd just (or hadn't even) met.

"Owen, I just woke up, so I'm going to stir around a little, and then I'll head your way. Can you get me an address?"

"Yeah, it'll be 300 Weaver Street. GPS should get you here just fine, if you aren't familiar yet."

"Perfect. I'll see you in an hour, hour and a half."

"Great. Thank you, Mr. Douglas."

Lakin was about to deposit the phone into his pocket when it buzzed again: a message containing a phone number for 'Chitto' from Shaw. He made a mental note to give him a call to meet up, maybe this evening. He didn't want to be up here in Rotten Fork all year looking for imaginary wolves; he wanted to get this sorted out as soon as possible. He'd follow all of the leads he could.

First though, he was going to meet Owen Mayer.

Lakin was puzzled as the GPS led him into the heart of the small town, somehow situated below the main road, with tall brick buildings that were mostly not in use. It was beyond the single strip of buildings he had seen on his first day there.

"In the middle of town?" he said to himself, turning his wheel down Weaver Street. The address belonged to a pawn shop, one that he imagined happily took stolen goods and probably sold drugs under the table. A man was standing outside of the door, and he would have bet on him being Owen Mayer before they even spoke.

"Mr. Douglas!"

Owen acted excited to see him, the enthusiasm of an old friend. He even moved in to hug him as he exited the vehicle. Lakin didn't rebuke him or pull away but allowed his arms to be trapped reluctantly against his trunk as the large man squeezed him tightly and wrapped him in an aroma of microwave burritos and value brand cologne that made Lakin think of the old phrase 'toilet water'.

"Just back this way," Owen said, guiding him around the side of the building. Lakin was relieved that they weren't going to go inside, as he suspected Owen was the type to offer a tour.

"I didn't expect an incident so close to so much activity," Lakin admitted.

"Oh, it's pretty quiet around back. Never seen anything like it. I've been doing this for twenty five years and never."

"Doing what?"

"Well, owning the store. Resaling, you know. Bartering, trading."

Lakin was unsure how the occupation was relevant, but he followed quietly all the same. As they rounded the back of the store, Lakin noted a hand-painted wooden pallet that said DONATIONS. Beneath it were two boxes full of pornographic DVDs, an old tube television, and a bag of stained clothes (torn open by what was probably a scavenging feral cat, looking for food in a familiar black trash liner).

Owen walked beyond that to a long patch of grass that was mostly overgrown, other than a few inconsistent strips and spots. It looked like it once had been a nice yard of some sort; perhaps the pawn shop had once been a residential building. Now, the old yard was just neglected.

"Do you see it? The patterns cut in the grass?"

Lakin opened his mouth to speak.

"I know what you're thinking..."

"I don't think you do..." he insisted quietly.

"And I'm thinking the same thing. Dead animals, missing animals, and now a gosh damned crop circle right behind my shop."

"Ah..!" Lakin said, suddenly understanding what he was supposed to be looking at.

Owen was looking at him now, red-faced and exasperated. "Alients."

"Aliens, of course."

They stared at each other and then the grass for several long seconds.

Then Lakin spoke again, "So, I don't think this is related to the animals."

"You don't?"

"No, I don't."

"Well, that makes me feel right stupid, Mr. Douglas."

Lakin shook his head side to side, smiling supportively, "I mean clearly this... this..."

"Crop circle."

"Crop circle is the work of some intelligent being. Higher thinking being."

"Yeah, clearly," Owen agreed, flush slowly leaving his face. "That's what I was thinking."

"But I'm here to look for an animal. So this... all of this, isn't really my jurisdiction. Above my paygrade, you know? You need a different kind of person for this."

"Like who?"

"I don't know, Mr. Mayer… Owen. I bet if you post online, somebody will come investigate for you."

"How much you think that'll cost me?"

"I have no idea."

"You mean the internet, right?"

"Yes, that's what I mean."

"So you just look at animals. You a vet? Cause I got a dog with a bald spot above his ass, itches so bad."

"No, I'm a biologist."

"Don't know what that is…" Owen muttered, trudging back towards the store.

"I'm sorry I wasn't more help."

Owen waved his hand over his shoulder, "Oh, it's alright. Thanks for coming out."

Lakin went back to his vehicle, sitting heavily in the seat. When the door was closed and he turned the key in the ignition, he caught himself laughing.

ii.

It had been his idea to move there, but she had not missed a beat when he suggested it. She had her bags packed before he'd even found them a place to live. She had always encouraged him and stayed faithfully by his side. Even as he struggled with work and as finances became increasingly terrifying, she was his sunshine. As the days grew dark, like they did, she was a warm brightness.

Constant.

He did not know that she was burning alive, smoldering until all the fuel would be used up. He didn't know that she needed something he could not give her, that no mortal could give her, that nothing in life could give her. She needed something to keep burning, but he didn't understand that until it was too late. He would have given anything to have realized it before he found her light snuffed out and her body cold, last remnants of heat leaving her mouth in visible swirls like the smoke from the extinguished flame of her soul.

six

The restaurant where he had agreed to meet Chitto was attached to an old general store. It was made of the original wood on the exterior, which added antique charm to the building from the road and parking lot. Inside, however, it had been lined with new materials that boasted of modernization. There was a row of glass-front cabinetry, filled with homemade fudge, and a classic soda fountain. It wasn't the type of place where Lakin would have chosen to eat. While he loved the small-town charm of a little café on a corner, this place was a little too touristy for him.

The warmth was inviting, though, and the aroma of food was pleasant. Chitto had specified to Lakin exactly where he would be seated, which was a table along the backside of the room and directly adjacent to a wall heater. Lakin loosened the scarf around his neck and removed his head covering, running his fingers through his mess of hair before he headed to the designated seat.

He saw a man sitting there, wearing a pair of too-tight jeans, black boots, and a nice taupe turtleneck shirt. His long hair was dark and braided down the center of his back. His fingernails were painted a bold teal. He didn't look like he belonged in a place like this, despite the way he chatted with people as they walked by, like every one of them knew him. He gave the last person a little time to walk away before he started across the room again.

Lakin approached hesitantly, leaning on the back of the free chair.

"Chitto?"

The man stood immediately, offering a hearty handshake which Lakin returned warmly with a smile.

"You must be Douglas."

"Lakin Douglas, yeah. Pleasure to meet you. That's a nice color on you," he said, motioning to his fingers. If a man was going to paint his nails such a shade, he wanted people to notice.

Chitto put his hand to his chest, fingers splayed for effect. "Why, thank you," he laughed. "My daughter is obsessed with nail polish right now. It's the thing. You should see my toes. She did them in Sugar Plumb Crazy."

Lakin relaxed into the chair, scooting against the table. It put him at ease how Chitto talked to him, smiling and belly laughing, like they had known each other for years before this encounter. He didn't even care if it was fake friendliness.

"So you're here to take down our secret treasures, huh?"

"I'm sorry?"

"The big bad wolves."

Lakin laughed quietly now, torn by the way Chitto had worded it. Clearly he believed they were there, too, but he also didn't seem to see them as pests like everyone else. He valued them.

Lakin shook his head from side to side. "Let me assure you, if there are wolves here... I'm going to advocate for them. But on the other side of that, if one really is acting out like this... it could become dangerous for the whole population. Sometimes it just takes one bad seed to convince everyone to start misbehaving."

Chitto had pulled his phone from his pocket, loading photos and laying it face up on the table as he turned it to face Lakin.

"Just swipe left for more."

Lakin was impressed. The photos of the paw prints were clear, well positioned, with measuring tools and notes on white paper with information of location, date, time, climate.

"This is really impressive," Lakin admitted. "It still isn't enough for me to cry wolf, so to speak, with such a pun, but it is definitely coming closer to convincing me that they're out there. The prints do suggest the possibility of a wolf and not a dog, judging by the way the front and rear prints are positioned in a line. That being said, I've still got to see them in the flesh to believe it."

He swiped again, seeing a large print, sloppy and splay-footed like it had been running. The measuring tool was the same as before, but it looked much smaller. Then he thought he could see the clear, long digits of human fingers pressed into the mud nearby.

"What are these?" Lakin asked, puzzled.

"Nothing," Chitto insisted, pulling the phone back to him. "Prints of something I hadn't seen before, never looked too hard into it."

"So, are the prints of the wolves in an area where I could easily, and legally, access?"

"Yeah, most of it is on my personal property. The wolves are there, they pass between my south boundary and the line of the Boyd homeplace."

"You've tracked them?"

"Seen them both places. Same pack."

Lakin was dubious, despite his inclination to trust the friendly man in front of him. Chitto seemed like more of a no-nonsense kind of guy but was also cordial.

"Alright then, I'll bite. When can I check it out?"

"You can follow me back there now, if you want."

"Not hungry?"

"Nah, I just meet people here to feel them out first. Never invite some stranger to your house," Chitto laughed. "Didn't your mama tell you that?"

Lakin started laughing with him. "So I passed the test? Don't think I'm a creep?"

"I didn't say that, I just decided I could take you if I had to," Chitto snarked playfully as he got up and started walking to the door. Lakin followed behind him.

The drive to Chitto's place was short and quiet. He had felt warm when he left the restaurant. Warm inside. Chitto was friendly and welcoming. He had one of those dispositions that relaxed you with faux familiarity. He'd probably make a good serial killer, Lakin told himself. After all, here he was driving out to his secluded home alone, none the wiser.

The house was just outside of town, on a road that Lakin had passed on his way in. He remembered seeing it because of the sagging mailbox that had caught the light from his headlights as he drove by. It appeared to have been hit, just barely clinging to its post and wavering in the breeze like a hanging body. Down a short dirt road that led over a steep hill, where the road gave birth to an overgrown yard, sat a little trailer that was not unlike the sagging mailbox.

Lakin would have been lying had he pretended that he wasn't surprised by the place where Chitto lived. The home sat directly on the ground with a spacious front porch full of windchimes and little decorations. There was a squeaking metal glider that clunked against the front of the house and a doghouse where a dog of some fluffy northern descent lazily slept inside with just its marbled pink-and-black nose sticking out.

Chitto stood outside of his Jeep, rubbing his hands together as though he was getting cold waiting on Lakin to get out. Lakin took his time, turning the old vehicle off before he put on a set of waterproof gloves and pulled his woolen cap down over his ears. He tucked his camera bag under his arm.

"Alright," Chitto said as Lakin approached, turning his back on him to point out to the treeline in the distance. "You're going to head south, and just keep your nose in that direction. You'll eventually come to a fence line that will have private property signs, all of that. That's the Boyd homestead. No one lives there right now, the Boyds moved off a couple of years ago. Their daughter had an accident, and they couldn't stand the place anymore. Property has been sitting there unattended, nobody checks in on it. If you have any problems, shoot me a message. You won't have enough service for any calls but should be able to get a text out."

"Thanks," Lakin said with a nod, staring off across the dim landscape.

"You got a gun on you?"

"Rifle's in the truck," Lakin said, motioning over his shoulder with his thumb.

"I recommend you take it with you. There's worse things than wolves to be worried about out there. Just to be safe."

He agreed with a nod, getting the rifle bag out and slinging it onto his free side before he stalked off across the yard. He crossed a single strand of barbed wire carefully, metal hovering just an inch from the seat of his pants as he stiffly pulled the opposite leg across.

This was what he loved about his job... at least, it used to be what he loved about it. The solitude of nature was now deafening. It was something that he could no longer return from. The loneliness followed him out of the forest and back into life. When Lena had been alive, it was something he was able to shed: taking it off with his boots and coat, heavy with the scent of a man who had been in the wilderness for days at a time, and he slipped back into some form of domestication. Comfortable communion, a placating partnership.

This was the first time he had been in the woods since she had left him. Even this forest that was unfamiliar to him somehow seemed like one he had been in a hundred times. The ground was soft underfoot. Startlingly green mosses seemed to have persevered beneath the melting snow, frozen and decaying polyphores clinging to the trees with oozing blackness.

The scents were what he might have missed the most. He found that his olfactory sense stimulated memory more than anything else, stirring something still warm in the ashes up to the surface again.

He followed Chitto's instruction, keeping his tracks dutifully south and a nervous eye on the lowering sun. A couple of hours of daylight remained, but soon would be the birth of dusk, when it was somehow harder to see than during pure night.

The rolling forest hills had started to level out, usually a sure sign that human development was to follow. He wasn't surprised when he could see an old fence in the distance, barely visible if not for the pink tape tied around a central strand of barbed wire, wooden posts reclaimed by lichen and insects. He was, however, more surprised when he noticed fresh scat on the ground and would have missed it if not for a bare area in the leaf litter. He squatted down, removing a glove to hold a bare palm over top, feeling warmth emanating from the stool.

"Never been so fascinated by a pile of shit..." he muttered, putting his glove back on as he followed the fence line east. The scat had certainly looked more wolf and less dog.

He rationalized that a dog that was exclusively eating wildlife or scavenging may have similar fecal content.

He came to an area where the fence had fallen, twisting on itself as it suspended in a low enough place to cross, yellow NO TRESPASSING sign flapping uselessly in the middle. Although Chitto had assured him this trek was safe, it still felt a little...

Well, illegal. It was still illegal, even if no one caught you. Lakin had done his fair share of illegal activities; who hadn't? But generally speaking, the laws he chose to break were often for what he considered to be the greater good.

He could see that he was on a small plateau of sorts now, almost having walked right off the edge of a moderately sized embankment. Several yards below and a half mile into the distance, he saw an old house. It was huge, which he could tell even from where he stood. An old, colonial style farmhouse that had once no doubt been beautiful. It was falling apart now, covered in invasive kudzu and graffiti.

In what had once been a courtyard, now no more than a grassy expanse dotted with cement adornments, Lakin saw movement. He slowly dropped to his knees, moving over to a log so that he could prop himself up and unpack his rifle. He whispered quietly to himself as he worked, not even aware of what his own lips were saying. It was like an arcane and ancient language, prose that formulated in moments like this.

He positioned the gun and peered through the sight, looking again for the source of movement near what had once been a fountain.

Lakin stared at the wolf through his sight on his rifle as it rejoined a group of maybe four or five other individuals. He was almost giddy with excitement. Gray wolves never had a natural territory in Tennessee. Red wolves were hunted to extinction, and even when they were bred in captivity and reintroduced, they were unable to thrive and fizzled out. These wolves he saw now were either red wolves or some comparable coyote-wolf hybrid. He wasn't sure.

But the point now was that he believed. What he didn't believe, however, was that these animals were killing livestock so prolifically.

He put the rifle to the side carefully, removing his camera quietly, and attaching the long zoom lens. The photos wouldn't be winning any awards, but they would serve as proof. Not proof for the sheriff and the townspeople, but proof for the scientific community. The rediscovery of these animals in this area was huge.

He took the shots he needed, removing the lens and placing it with great care back into the case. He would have lain there to watch the wolves for hours, had it not been so close to nightfall and had he not left his vehicle at Chitto's. This was an experience only comparable to encountering a unicorn. In this case, a small herd of unicorns.

He stole one glance back at the animals, as they slunk away into the tall grasses, and began heading down the fence line again. Instead of crossing back where he had before, he followed the barbed wire down to what he thought would have been the front of the property. He was curious to see which highway or major backroad the property was adjacent to. He kept the long driveway, still identifiable through the overgrowth, to his left and the fence to his right.

Dusk started to fall, sneaking a haze onto the world. Ahead of him, in the fading light, Lakin thought he saw a figure against a fence post. He hesitated, heart fluttering in his chest. He wasn't sure why it unsettled him, but there was something about running into a person in the middle of nowhere that was unnatural. Like he somehow belonged here, but other people... so often, they didn't. He smiled and shouldered his rifle, trying to make it clear that he had no intention of using it right now.

"Hello," he called. "My name is Lakin Douglas. I'm here with permission from Chitto. I know this isn't his property but..."

His appeasing smile faded as he squinted at the figure, realizing that it had not responded to his voice or presence. The hair stood on the back of his neck as he headed forward. As the figure came into view, he noted that it wasn't a person at all.

Lakin didn't want to acknowledge that what he was seeing was really there. On a rotten fence post, the hollowed out and decaying head of a goat stood out like an effigy. Flies were swarming what meat was still left on the bone, eyes missing and replaced with pulsing white larvae. It wasn't the goat's head that disturbed him, or even the fact that between its two impressive horns sat what he assumed was the skull of the missing dog. It was the confirmation that this was not the work of an animal. This was not his job. It was not his expertise. Give him a rogue wolf or a brave puma any day. Rabid foxes or racoons in an attic. A problem bear who had learned that people have the best food. This was not something he wanted to deal with. He would rather go look into Owen Mayer's aliens for him. Pro bono.

He snapped photos from every angle and then started looking for those human footprints he had seen before. That was when he noticed the large, deep indentations on the other side of the fence. The human prints were there, but there was something else. Something canine, but far too massive for the small wolves he had just observed.

And much larger than any other canine he knew to still exist.

seven

Lakin paced around the cabin's small floor, tidying like a nervous teenager before his date showed up. He made sure the bed was made, laptop set up on the table with the photographs pulled up. He ran his hand through his hair as he looked around the room, realizing that he was sweating.

"Just calm down," Lakin told himself. "Just calm down. Show him what you've found. Focus on that."

Chitto had been surprised when Lakin came sprinting out of the woods, pale faced and panicked. He told him he'd talk to him later and that he didn't have time to explain. Even though Chitto had just met him, he seemed to realize how uncharacteristic this rush was for Lakin. He just nodded, wishing him well and going on inside. With a smile and a wave, he disappeared behind a slamming screen door.

He heard a car pull near the cabin and stop, engine idling loudly. He thought he could identify the miss in the engine as one that belonged to Shaw's truck. He exhaled in relief, opening the door before Shaw ever knocked.

The sheriff stood outside with a surprised gleam in his eye, fist poised to knock on the wood.

"Well, aren't you eager this evening?" he laughed. "So what's all the excitement, Lakin? I hope this is good. Tonight is date night."

"I hate to get between you spending time with your wife, Mr. Lowell. I just have something I want you to see. Something I think you need to see."

He ushered Shaw inside, clicking the photo of the skulls on the fence post and blowing it up to full size. Lakin put his hand to his mouth as he looked down at it. He could almost hear and smell the photo. Shaw squinted at it, leaning onto the table with one hand, other hand gently tapping the mouse to scroll through the pics.

He didn't stop, however, until he came to one of the photos of the red wolf. He smiled and motioned toward the screen. "Told you. There they are... little bastards."

Lakin was perturbed. He even jerked his head back and blinked wildly. "Did you not see..." He tapped the arrow aggressively until the skulls reappeared. "This?"

Shaw pulled his lower lip between his teeth, biting down. He looked at the photo for several minutes before responding, "You know, I'm just not one hundred percent sure what I'm looking at here, Lakin."

Lakin pointed at the lower skull first. "This is the skull of a goat, and here on top... this is canine. I think this is both the missing goat and the missing livestock dog from the Simms property."

"What makes you think that?"

"Well, I mean... what are the odds?"

"The odds of what exactly?" Shaw asked, standing up now and crossing his arms over his chest.

"Of someone killing these two animals and arranging their heads like this. This was someone sending a message."

"I thought you were supposed to be looking for the animal that killed this goat? The wolves that you have claimed didn't exist here. But now I see that you know they are here."

He seemed satisfied with himself as he spoke. Lakin wondered if Shaw said things in that manner to try to push his buttons. He had never before felt so targeted by someone's behavior.

"Where did you find these skulls?" Shaw asked, making a face when he said the final word, as though there were any question as to what Lakin had photographic evidence of.

"I don't know why you're saying it like that... It was clearly two half-rotting skulls stacked together like some kind of weird totem in the middle of the..."

Shaw tilted his head at him, raising his brows and frowning like one would toward a stubborn child. "Where did you find them?"

"I don't know... on the border of some old homestead. Boyd, I think."

"Ah, the Boyd Place. Not surprising. You do know that's private property right? Yeesh... can't just walk around like you own the place, Lakin."

"I'm just... Listen. I know you want to pin all of this on the wolves but... an animal couldn't... wouldn't do this," Lakin insisted.

"So you are really suggesting someone from the Fork is behind all of this?"

"Maybe some kids."

"You think kids are killing livestock?"

"Teenagers. Maybe they're acting out, looking for attention."

"I don't really understand why you keep deflecting your responsibilities, Lakin."

"This is your responsibility, Mr. Lowell. There are human footprints, I have photos."

Shaw took a step towards him, smiling with white teeth through his full beard. "You're here to catch an animal. I'm starting to wonder if you'd recognize one if it was standing right in front of you."

Lakin took a step backwards before he realized it, catching himself mid stride, which only caused an awkward bounce on his heel as he rocked forward to meet Shaw's advancement. "I just don't think this is an animal. At first I thought that it could be dogs, but now I think... no, I know that someone is behind this."

Shaw briefly looked Lakin up and down. Lakin swallowed nervously, attempting to hold his ground. Shaw finally laughed, holding his hands up as a truce. "That was out of line of me, wasn't it? Rude. I just don't want you to end up hurt out here, you know? Coming in, blaming local people..."

Lakin swallowed, cotton mouth nearly choking him on his own tongue as it clung to his hard palate. When he finally found his voice, it was low and rumbling, barely audible. He felt a nervous quiver in his gut that rattled in his chest as it rose. "I don't mean to be confrontational... but are you threatening me, Mr. Lowell?"

Shaw shook his head, calmly putting his hand on Lakin's shoulder, "No, I'm not. I'm not threatening you. I'm just telling you, if you go around making claims... pointing fingers... don't be surprised when people bite back. Oh, and one more thing. I keep telling you to call me Shaw. Please."

"Okay," Lakin whispered. It was the only word he could find the bravery to mutter. This interaction today had not gone as planned, at all.

"Thanks, it's really pissing me off that I have to keep asking."

eight

Lakin had thought that Shaw would never leave after the awkward exchange. He had an unsettled feeling about the situation, and he thought that it might be best for him to just cut his losses and get out of there. He knew that those red wolves had likely never preyed on any livestock or pets. He also knew that the locals wanted answers, and it was easier for a small-time sheriff who didn't even live in this town to throw blame on a wild animal than to try to put a human face to the turmoil and deal with the public. He could understand that.

"You need to tell him that," Lakin said quietly to himself. "Tell him you get it, but tell him you just can't give him any proof an animal performed the attacks. Move on. Tell him you're sorry you weren't more help, and go home."

But he didn't want to go home. The Lowell cabin was somehow just familiar enough.

There was a scratching at the door, something that he was immediately attentive to. He wondered if a mouse had found its way inside and was scurrying around near the walls.

As he approached the door, however, he heard the quietest mewling from the opposite side. It was a sound that most certainly belonged to a cat, and so Lakin cracked the door open to peek out.

Sitting in the snow, tail curled around to cover his white-tipped toes, the cat looked up at him expectantly. Its green eyes were lazy-looking, a low brow that caused the cat to look like it was skeptical or tired. It chattered at him, voice husky and hoarse. It looked down at his feet and back up at his face, as though asking if he were going to invite him inside.

Without hesitation, Lakin let the cat into the cabin. He was somehow sure that Shaw was not a cat person and would probably have insisted that there be no cat sleepovers. This made him want to let the cat sleep inside even more.

It shook off its orange feet, stretching and quivering from nose to tail as it moved to knead the stone in front of the fire. It acted like it knew where the warmth came from and that it was accustomed to being inside.

He liked cats. He hated that they were so often left outside to their own devices, people coming up with the excuse that they needed the wild. They were a destructive force: a cunning and highly efficient predator that killed for fun. For a biologist like Lakin, they were a nightmare that could wreak serious havoc on an ecosystem of small animals... creatures that people often didn't even know existed. Insects, small birds, amphibians, reptiles, moles, shrews. All of these animals were helpless against a bored house cat.

But at the end of the day, he wasn't waging war on little red cats.

He lay in the bed, getting under the covers and laughing as the cat hopped onto the bed with him, trilling. It approached briefly, sharp nails digging into his thighs as it presented its crown to be petted. He obliged, scratching behind its ears as its head swiveled to take advantage of as much contact as possible. Lakin then thumbed the copper disk on the collar around its neck, which was heavily worn and scuffed. It read REGRET, with no contact information.

The cat moved down to the end of the bed and lay on top of his ankles, tucking its feet underneath itself and closing its eyes. He could feel the gentle vibrations of its purr against his skin, even through the blankets.

He slept better than he had in weeks. In fact, he didn't remember falling asleep; he was just suddenly consumed by a dreamless rest. Not until he was woken the next morning by the sounds of the cat yowling and pawing at the window, knocking everything off that it could as it tried to get out, did he realize how deeply he had fallen into sleep. He blinked away grogginess, struggling to his feet as he opened the front door.

The cat darted out.

As he closed the door and passed by the window, he caught sight of someone walking down the highway. He would not have thought much about it, but they were staggering, and he could tell that they were not dressed for the weather... in fact, at first he thought they were nude. He squinted through the fogged glass, and then he realized it was Marie Baldwin.

Lakin snatched his coat and threw on his long johns and boots, running up the hill to the road, where Marie had already passed by and continued walking. She wore nothing but a thin nightgown, shorter than knee length, with slim straps across the shoulders and barely enough frilled fabric to modestly cover her breasts.

"Mrs. Baldwin," Lakin called after her, looking both ways down the asphalt before he went after her.

"Marie," he said, starting to jog so that he could catch up to her. He started to wonder if it was actually her, judging by the way she did not even slightly respond to her name.

As he approached, he noticed she was bleeding, hands covered in red. Had she been in an accident? Was she disoriented from a head injury? Lakin would normally not touch a woman without her explicit permission, but she did not stop walking. He grabbed her by the elbow, saying her name again as he gently turned her towards him. He was surprised when she spun at him aggressively, pounding her bloody fists into his chest over and over again.

"Marie! Marie, Jesus Christ..." she was knocking the breath out of him as she screamed, continuing to swing at him as he tried to back away from her furious strikes.

He caught both of her wrists, crossing them against her own chest, "Marie, it's me, Lakin Douglas. I'm staying at Shaw's Cabin. Remember? You brought me a delicious casserole the fist night I was here. Do you remember that, Marie? Are you okay? Were you in a car accident? Where are you hurt?"

She suddenly stared at him, lower lip quivering, blue eyes rimmed by pink, pallid horror. "He's dead. He's dead. He killed him."

Lakin chewed his thumbnail nervously as he sat in the chair at the Baldwins' residence. He hadn't wanted to come here. He wasn't sure why he didn't say 'no' when Shaw told him to get in. He was such a yes-man. Always a yes-man. He remembered Lena telling him he had to set boundaries to protect himself, that he was too nice. No one wanted to think of themselves as a doormat, as someone who allowed people to just walk all over them, but here Lakin was somewhere he didn't want to be. All because he didn't want to say no, when it was a completely reasonable response to the situation at hand.

Shaw came back into the house, and Lakin sat up in his seat, pressing his palms against his knees,

"She okay?" Lakin asked, voice quiet.

Shaw sighed, "Marie? Yeah... she'll be alright. They're taking her to the hospital to get checked out, but she'll be fine, I think. Pretty sure all of the blood was Tony's."

"What was she doing out on the highway? Why didn't she call somebody?" They were questions that Lakin didn't expect an answer to. He was just too overwhelmed by the situation at hand to say anything else.

"Shock, I guess. Lucky you saw her. If you hadn't been staying at the cabin, she might've wandered down into the woods or gotten hit by a car... Who knows."

"Yeah... lucky." It didn't seem like the right word. No one was lucky in this scenario.

"Come look at something for me." Shaw motioned to Lakin who, of course, followed. They went outside, walking through the small crowd of people that had gathered. Some of them were medical professionals, it looked like, and some were other cops. Maybe even a few civilians: people walking around in plain clothes who seemed too calm to be at a crime scene.

The body of Tony Baldwin lay in the slush on the ground, on his back.

"What do you think?"

Lakin had his hand over his mouth, which was slightly ajar. He didn't know how you got used to seeing people like this.

"What?" Lakin asked quietly. Why was Shaw asking his opinion on this? Why couldn't he turn away from the man's body on the ground? He thought he was going to be sick.

Shaw scoffed, crossing his arms over his chest. "Animal attack? You're the expert."

Lakin stammered, "What? No... I mean, I don't think so... no."

Tony's face was gone. His neck was a gully that led to the crater where his nose once was. There were still pieces of teeth sticking out of the bloody pulp: the only remnants of a mouth at all. He couldn't imagine that an animal had done this. He did note that Tony's fingernails were broken and bloody, but there were no defensive wounds on his arms or legs. How would an animal go straight for the face and throat, with no damage anywhere else? And better yet, why would it? He wanted to say these things, but he couldn't.

"Suicide then?" Shaw stated with a shrug.

Lakin shook his head. "What would cause that much damage?"

"Don't act like you don't know the damage a gun can do at close range, Lakin."

Lakin's ears started ringing, and his gut felt cold. His head was swimming wildly, and he felt himself swaying on his feet. He didn't blink, fearing that if he did he would hit the ground.

"What did you say to me?" he asked, voice barely a breath.

"You..."

Lakin had punched Shaw in the mouth before he realized it. He pulled his arm back like it had acted on its own, spinning away to start walking down the Baldwin's driveway. He heard someone yell at him, but Shaw told the man to leave it.

If Marie Baldwin could walk to the cabin barefoot in a nightgown, he could get there in his boots.

nine

Lakin was packing his bag at the cabin when there was a knock. His stomach sank to the soles of his feet, pulling on something in the back of his throat. Was it Shaw coming to arrest him? Or worse, to confront him in that weird and somehow polite way? He decided to not even go to the door, continuing to shove his meager belongings away. The knocking came again soon after, and he heard a soft voice say his name.

He paused. It wasn't Shaw's voice, but instead another man's. He recognized it, somehow, and it took him a few minutes to put a face to the voice. There was another small knock, and Lakin slowly walked over to the entrance. He checked outside the window first, just glimpsing the back of someone's head and shoulders, the heels of their boots on the welcome mat.

He cracked the door open suspiciously, peering out to see Chitto standing in the snow in a green turtleneck.

"I come in peace," Chitto said with a smile, holding up two six packs of beer.

Lakin let him in, ushering the cold back out by rapidly closing the door. Chitto entered, seating himself on the chair near the small loveseat. He seemed to know the cabin and was familiar with the way it was laid out, much like Marie and the orange cat had been.

"I guess you heard," Lakin said, awkwardly fidgeting before he too had a seat.

"That you have a hell of a right hook for a tree hugger? Yeah, I heard."

He pulled one of the cans off of the plastic ring and handed it to him. It looked like a cheap beer, and subsequently it smelled and tasted like cheap beer: the slightly soured and bitter flavor of acid reflux in aluminum. But it served its purpose. Lakin had never been much of a drinker, although he would have a drink with friends at work whenever he was invited. It mostly involved babysitting a glass of blonde, nursing the foam all night while you watched sports on the bar television. No one kept count of how much you drank, and by the end of the night you were claiming that your first glass was your third and you had better cash out your tab.

Chitto pressed on in the silence, "So what happened?"

Lakin didn't know how to answer that. He didn't know how to tell Chitto that Shaw had been on his bad side since he'd arrived. They had just gotten off on the wrong foot and continued hopping on that bad leg until they toppled over.

That this had been building up for a while, and how what had happened earlier was just the last straw.

"He made a comment."

Chitto sipped his beer, staring at Lakin patiently. This is why he was that somebody who knew something about everybody.

"He made a comment about me knowing what guns did at close range. That's exactly what he said to me."

Chitto looked puzzled. "I'm not following."

"My wife committed suicide." Lakin swallowed, eyes burning. Chitto blew air sharply out of his pursed lips in response to the admission, and Lakin went on, "She did it with my handgun."

Chitto squeezed the can a little too hard, thumb making an indention in the side. "Oh, shit, Lakin. I'm sorry. I had no idea; no one had any idea. I don't think Shaw has any idea either. We knew you'd lost her, but not how."

"The way he said it and the way he looked at me."

"How would he have known?"

Lakin buried his fingers in his hair, using the heel of his hand to apply pressure to his forehead.

"I don't know. Jesus. I don't know. You're right, aren't you? He didn't know... I just punched a man. Assault. A police officer. "

"It's alright. Just... calm down. It's going to be okay."

"No, it isn't. I'm losing it. I did this to get my mind off of losing her. And it's all I think about. She's everywhere."

"I know. You're taking on a lot right now, brother."

"I saw the wolves, just like you said. I found them, but there was something else up there."

"Something else?"

"I found a goat and dog skull stacked on a fence post."

"Well, that's..." Chitto burped under his breath. "Peculiar."

"A Simms man was missing a goat and a dog. I think it was them. Shaw still wants me to pin this all on an animal. He even had the nerve to ask me if it looked like Tony might have been attacked by an animal. You'd think that he'd want to find out what happened to him, instead of just pinning it on an animal."

"You didn't hear this from me... but Shaw and Tony had bad blood, you see."

"Bad blood?"

"Shaw had an affair with a girl named Holly Gernt. You met her yet?"

"No. Not that I can recall."

"Well, anyway. It's common knowledge in town that he did."

"Stepped out on Mrs. Lowell? She seems like..." Lakin paused for the right word, tapping his foot on the floor once. "A really nice lady. Wouldn't have thought that."

Chitto agreed with a nod, "Nobody's perfect, Claire included. I hear she hasn't been completely faithful either. So then there were rumors that Shaw also slept with Marie Baldwin. Marie's really friendly, you know and Shaw has always been really good to Marie and her family, and he's even gotten Tony out of some shit before... for the sake of Marie and the boys, mostly. From what I hear, the whole thing about her and Shaw having an affair and all: that's bullshit. But it didn't matter when Tony heard about it. He beat the shit out of her. I guess he does that a lot, but this time he had an excuse to really lay it on her. She called 911, sounded so bad on the phone that they thought she'd had a stroke."

"Christ..." Lakin breathed.

"When the paramedics and Shaw showed up, it was clear what had happened. Tony drunk off his ass and raving about her being a whore... so then Shaw beat the shit out of him, which didn't help with the rumors but we all know he deserved it. So yeah, Shaw could probably give a rat's ass that Tony's dead. In fact, most of us couldn't care less."

"I get that he's a lowlife. I see that. But shouldn't someone less involved be investigating?"

"Somebody like who? We're lucky we have Shaw in town. Nobody else is going to come out here. Not for some abusive drunk ending up dead. We've had unsolved cases of good people. People who deserved some kind of special attention, outside attention. But places like this don't get that kind of outreach, not usually."

"Are there no other deputies in Last Bend?"

"Yeah, but they're stretched pretty thin on their own. It was pretty much an unwritten rule that Shaw would handle anything down this way. He insisted, I think."

"Why would he put that all on himself?" Lakin asked.

"He's lived here his entire life. I guess he feels a sense of duty. Or obligation."

Or he wants to be able to cover everything up when necessary, he thought. This only made Lakin more suspicious and less trusting of Shaw.

"Listen," Chitto said, leaning forward. "Don't rush off just yet. Even if you are fed up with the place. At least get paid. Tell Shaw you found the wolves, come up with some story about them migrating out of the Fork... He isn't going to check into it. Just give him what he wants and go home."

"I can't do that..." Lakin insisted. "I can't lie about that. I need to do a report on the location, I need to get permits to set up protected territory... This is a huge scientific discovery. I'm sure you know that. You knew they were special.

I could tell by the way you talked about them. I don't know if they're red wolves or a hybrid or what yet... but they shouldn't be here. They're thriving. This is significant."

"No, I understand. Not in the same way you do, but I do understand. The people who live here have known the wolves have been here forever. A lot of the older locals call them midlem. Which came from them once being called middlemen. Seems silly, I know." Chitto broke off another can and cracked it open, drinking it like it was water. Lakin took it upon himself to finish his and try to keep up. "You ever heard of psychopomps?"

Lakin thought that the word sounded familiar, but he couldn't place any kind of significance to it. It sounded like a made up word, or maybe the name of a band that played for tips and sang songs about horror movies and politics. He shook his head no instead, drinking his beer quietly.

"Messengers of the dead, you know. Of the afterlife. They say that those animals, the psychopomps, will appear to transport souls from this life to the next one. Some people think it's birds or foxes or cats or whatever. The wolves around here were always thought of as those middlemen, or as the hillbillies call them: midlem. I guess because it was so rare to see one and so many people that aren't from here refuse to believe they exist. Myth status."

"It's interesting," Lakin admitted. "But it still stands that I can't lie about them being out of the county if I want to hope to get a team in here later. I can't risk my reputation like that."

"Then you better be figuring out what your scapegoat is going to be," Chitto said, standing up and heading towards the door. "Unless you're really determined to get out of here right now."

Lakin fumbled with the can in his hand, watching as Chitto turned the knob and started out the door.

"What if I think it's somebody and not something?"

Chitto paused and looked back at him.

ten

Lakin had calmed down some after his chat with
Chitto the day before. For now he had decided to stay, even if it
was because he wanted to prove a person was up to all of the
mischief in Rotten Fork. He hadn't slept that night, turning
into bed much earlier than he usually did. He dreamed about
Tony's blown-off face. The gushing chasm that was his missing
sinuses and throat. He tried to blink away the vision, but
instead it kaleidoscoped into images of iron-rich stone,
blood-red rivers that cut through banks of snow.

In the middle of the night, or perhaps early morning,
Lakin awoke to a cold draft rolling through the cabin. It
seemed to cut through the bone, slipping under the blankets
and into every orifice. He felt himself draw together, trying to
conserve warmth at his core, and then he awoke. Somehow he
knew this had to be that dreaded witching hour. It was likely
because he had gone to sleep so early. His body had set up a
clock, and it decided it was time to get up and start the day. He
opened his eyes and sat bolt upright, bare shoulders stinging in

the sudden cold inside the building. He exhaled like a reverse gasp, breath bursting into a cloud of vapor in front of him. He almost thought he could see tiny crystals form from the moisture and fall like glittering shards onto the blanket that had slipped down around his waist.

The room was aglow with blue, and with the dark recesses around the walls it seemed to expand around him. In the center of the room but somehow yards away, a white light seemed to shine down from the ceiling. There was something there, a crumpled figure that stood maybe waist high. Was it snowing? Why was it snowing inside the cabin?

He was dreaming, wasn't he? It was the only explanation as the cabin's interior seemed to fade away and give entirely into the desolate snowscape. The absence of both heat and sound that one would not think of as quantitative but was somehow an infinite expanse of nothing but cold and quiet that lay just beyond measurable grasp. It was heavy, dense, suffocating even in its crisp sharpness.

He forced himself to his feet. The feeling of burning cold on the soles of his feet sent a wave of discomfort coursing across his entire body and covered him in gooseflesh. He walked towards the figure in the center of the room, briefly wondering if he was approaching at all. He could hear the crunch of snow under his bare feet, almost as though he were wearing his boots, the pleasant sound of packed snow grunting and squeaking underfoot. It seemed like the thing never got closer, no matter how long he trudged towards it... and then, slowly, it did start to grow larger, nearer.

Soon he was within close enough proximity that he could have touched it, but he didn't. Instead, he slowly walked around it, approaching the back of the thing. He could not shake the feeling that it was something he recognized. It was intentionally dark there, although it was washed in light, he thought. Strange how the mind delivered things sometimes.

He was behind it. The piled thing leaned forward to make a sort of overhang. He also leaned forward, looking down now to see that it had a large hole through it, one that allowed light to filter all the way to the snow beneath.

With a sizzling noise, almost like static, the hole closed itself back up. It was a slow process, tendrils of something crawling across to fill back in. As it closed another sound started coming from the object, and he started to shake. A racking sob that vibrated him to his core because it was then that he realized. He realized all at once what he was looking at, looking into. He remembered the sound of crying, the way that it sounded more painful and pitiful than anything he had ever heard. It brought him back to that moment. He realized what it was, who it was.

Lena sat upright and put the gun in her mouth in one fluid movement, like she had done it a million times in this purgatory. He was sprayed with blood and tissue as she opened the hole again, a fleshy flower exploding on the back of her skull: blooming into something terrible with red petals and tendrils of white and black.

Lakin sat up in bed, screaming. He could feel his heart pounding in his chest and ringing in his ears like a steady tone. The room was warm, almost unbearably so. He reached up to feel his face, the wetness on his skin almost making him sick at first until he realized it was sweat.

It wasn't like he had woken up from a dream; it was as though he had been blown back into his body with the bullet that passed through her brain. It felt too real.

"Breathe," Lakin whispered. "What the fuck. Just a nightmare. Breathe."

He told himself: you've got a lot going on. He needed to find something to do today. He couldn't sit here. Maybe he would run to the store and get something to take to Marie Baldwin, an excuse to talk to her about Tony and about Shaw. She had brought him a casserole when he first came here, so maybe he could return the favor (with something less homemade, of course).

Shaw wouldn't like it. If he heard about Lakin snooping around down there, especially after their little altercation, things could go south pretty quickly. He was surprised that the sheriff hadn't shown back up at the cabin already. It was his property after all.

He put on the same clothes he'd worn the day before and snatched his keys off of the table. It was funny how you had to be in a certain mood to 'get ready' for the day. Sometimes you just had to go at it without any preparation.

The car was cool inside but not as cold as it had been. Global warming, he figured. He turned on the heat long enough to defog the window before he pulled out onto the highway and started the short drive to the Fresh Mart in town.

The radio droned on with an old fashioned love song. He wondered how one-sided the song might be: the guy singing about the girl who broke his heart, spinning her like a siren who led him to ruin. No one talked about how the men had the choice but still set their sails towards the rocks.

He almost flipped the station, or at least reached to turn the arrow on the dial towards the floor, when the local station interrupted for a bulletin. At first Lakin thought that it might be a weather advisory. The snow had perhaps closed a business temporarily or delayed some sort of event. Although, as far as he could tell from the roads, it was mostly slush and water now. He figured the deeper back roads and shady embankments would continue to harbor snow and frost for weeks to come.

The announcer sounded haggard, like he hadn't been sleeping well. His voice carried such a thick accent that Lakin had some trouble understanding what he was saying, even without the clear fatigue that dripped from every word.

"We are still asking the community to keep their eyes open for any signs of Miss Dulcie Lloyd. The reward for any information that leads to her whereabouts is now at ten thousand dollars. Dulcie was reportedly last seen in her backyard at home but has been known to play in the woods in the property surrounding. As of right now, there has been no reason to suspect foul play... We are all just hoping, as a community, that Dulcie has wandered away and is waiting for someone to find her. We are remaining optimistic and are praying for the Lloyd family."

Lakin pressed the off button on the radio, listening to the engine and tires on the road instead. He didn't know who the Lloyd girl was, or how long she'd been missing at this point, but that sort of thing always made him uneasy. People just... disappearing without a trace. Especially children. Where were her parents when she disappeared? How did no one know where she went?

He tried to busy himself with happy thoughts, but those things seemed so elusive. His mind procured images of pheasant bursting out of a fall field, the soft smell of smoke on the air mingled with the aroma of wet dog: that faithful retriever going to fetch the felled bird for you. Maybe he needed a dog after all of this. Something to take care of. He might start with a houseplant first.

He pulled into the mostly empty parking lot of the Fresh Mart, parking as close to the front doors as possible. He shoved his hands deep into his pockets as he entered. An older gentleman stood near the cashier's station, sweeping the floor with a straw broom. The man nodded at him, head shaking involuntarily on top of his thin neck.

Lakin stopped by the deli section, where a long glass case of fresh meats ready for slicing were laid out before him. There were also pans of pre-prepared sides and other items you would usually associate with a catering service. He passed by a pan of something white and fluffy, with chocolate cookies on top.

"Excuse me," Lakin called to a woman behind the counter. She wore a hair net, black curls peeking out from beneath the elastic corners. She sat with her backside propped up against the cutting board surface of the counter top. She chewed gum loudly with her mouth open, glaring at him through dark eyes. She had a phone in her hand, thumb poised now over the screen as though he had interrupted something that just could not wait.

"Yeah?" she asked, voice annoyed.

"What is this?" he pointed, finger accidentally bouncing against the glass.

She walked over, looking down. "Tater salad."

"No. Next to it."

"Ah, oreo pudding. It's good, they say."

"Can I get some of that to go, please," Lakin asked politely, pulling his debit card out of his wallet.

"How much do you want?"

"Uh... Just give me enough for four."

He watched as the woman scooped four hefty spoonfuls of the pudding into a large container and then bagged it up, ringing him up for so little that he swapped the debit card for cash. He didn't know for sure how many children Marie Baldwin had, but he had heard her mention children the first day they'd met. He just hoped four servings would be enough.

The trip to Marie's from the store was slower than it should have been. Lakin twice turned down the wrong road on his way there. In his defense, he had only been to the house once, and that had been in the delirium of shock with Shaw and Marie as they returned to her home to find Tony dead in the yard. He could see it now, though, across the long gravel driveway that was adjacent to a stagnant pond.

He parked his car next to the old truck in the driveway and walked hesitantly up the stairs to the front door. The yard was eerily quiet. The wind blew a set of chimes and a suncatcher hanging from the porch covering, but they didn't seem to make a sound.

He rolled his knuckles against the storm door, feeling that even unlatching it to reveal the main door underneath was too intrusive. Marie opened it almost immediately, like she had been standing and waiting on the other side. He supposed that she might have seen his car pull up into the driveway, which was a long enough stretch that she could've heard the tires on gravel several minutes before he actually arrived.

She looked stressed but somehow less tired than she had the first time they'd met. Almost as though she had been able to sleep better lately. He wondered how you coped with that, when the loss of someone was a relief in so many ways.

"Marie," Lakin said quietly, holding the tub of pudding awkwardly against his gut. "I just wanted to come by and check up on you. I brought some of that cookie pudding from the Fresh Mart, for you and the kids. I thought... I don't know. I guess I thought sweets never made a situation worse."

She laughed, running a hand underneath both eyes as though she might have started to cry again had not the well run dry. She opened the door and motioned him inside.

"Come in and sit. The boys are at my mama's. I just... I needed some time to get things worked out. It was better for them to be away from home while I worked through it, I think.

They'll love that pudding though. They used to always beg for it when we'd go to the store. Tony never would budge..."

She took the container and set it inside the refrigerator: a large and yellowed box that looked like it was twice as old as the woman who was using it. She led him into the living room, where there was equally dated furniture, fraying carpet, and an old tube television on a peeling wood composite stand.

"Take a seat," she whispered, collapsing onto the couch.

Lakin sat carefully on the mustard and bronze armchair, thinking that he could immediately smell the musty odor of antique cushions and cigarette smoke puffing up like spores from a mushroom.

"I'm glad you came by. I wanted to... apologize." She stopped short, choking on the word.

"Marie, no," he said earnestly, leaning forward. "Don't apologize to me, please. You were in shock."

"I don't remember getting on the road. I don't remember anything."

"Grief... it'll do that to you. I understand. Trust me, I understand the crazy things it can do to your head. You don't have to explain anything to me."

"I've been trying to come to terms with it. I had this moment..." She twisted her hand in the air like she'd caught something there, fingers squeezing together. "I had this moment where I thought someone had killed him. Tony would never kill himself. Trust me. He was a drunk and an asshole, but he wasn't suicidal. I had this moment where I thought someone had killed him, and I knew who it was. So I think I panicked. I was scared. But then they say it looks like he might've been cleaning his gun maybe. They found a rag there, greasy. I'm just glad the boys weren't with him. What if he'd... He could've... I can't think about it."

"I'm sorry you and the boys are going through this. It must be so terrible..."

"It's the best thing," she whispered, and he saw the muscle in her jaw tighten. "It's going to be the best thing that ever happened to us."

She looked at him wide-eyed, tears bulging at the corners as fat droplets rolled down her cheeks. She looked crazed, insane, out of her head. It was like she dared him to confront her. He wouldn't. No woman deserved to be beaten, much less by a man who claimed to love her.

"Then I'm happy for you," he whispered back.

"I didn't do it. There was some people that thought that maybe I did it, because Tony had been so bad lately. I should've left, but I felt like I deserved it... even though I didn't do anything. I assume you've heard the rumors because nobody around here can keep their nose in their own business and keep their mouths shut... but I didn't sleep with Shaw. I know Tony thought I did, but I didn't. I swear on my babies' lives I never did."

"That's none of my business. It's none of anyone's business."

"I thought about it. I probably could have. I felt guilty even thinking of it though, even with Tony being the way he was, I still guilted myself over thinking of it. There was a night that my car wouldn't start and Shaw gave me a ride home. I could've, I think. He would've... I think."

Lakin shifted uneasily.

"I don't know why I'm telling you this," she admitted, also moving around in her seat. He thought he could see the muscles in her throat constrict, flesh pulling up off of her collar bone as she scrunched her face into another pained expression. "I just feel like someone needs to know in case... something happens. I didn't do it. I'm afraid of Shaw, too. Not in the same way I was afraid of Tony. I'm afraid of Shaw Lowell in... different ways. Does that make sense, Mr. Douglas?"

Lakin nodded slowly. "Yeah, it does."

Nothing made more sense. It comforted him somehow to know that he was not the only one who had felt the intimidation. The way the man seemed to be threatening even when he was friendly and jovial.

"Shaw and Claire have been together for years. Since they were kids. Claire's family moved into town and... well, you know it can be hard to move into a town like this one when you don't know anyone. They were total outsiders, and they weren't... they weren't friendly. Well, I guess it wasn't that they were unfriendly, they were just quiet. Claire had some kind of autoimmune disorder or something, I guess. They kept her inside most of the time. Lots of rumors about them because of that. Nasty rumors. Honestly no one saw much of her until she was nearly a teenager, and her and Shaw..."

She snapped her fingers then intertwined her index and middle finger together. "Just like that: inseparable."

"She got better, I guess?"

"What?"

"Claire. You said they kept her inside because of an autoimmune disorder."

Briefly Marie looked lost, eyes suddenly puffy and glazed. Then she inhaled, audibly, "Oh, yeah. They moved here for the fresh air they said. They said it was the best thing for her, she was cured. She's never been sick a day I've known her. No health issues other than they never could have kids. I mean, that's what people say. Maybe they didn't want any."

Lakin sighed, "Well, I better head back to the cabin... I just wanted to check on you. Make sure you were holding up okay."

"Thank you, Mr. Douglas. That means so much to me."

She walked him outside, standing on the porch as he walked to his vehicle. He passed through the yard and struck something in the dirt with his boot. He stopped, looking back over his shoulder to see Marie still watching. Lakin reached down and pulled the flesh-colored thing out of the dirt, finding a submerged plastic doll.

He raised it with a smile, showing her what he'd nearly tripped on and laid it in the grass instead.

"So sorry about that," she called. "That was Dulcie Lloyd's... Have you heard? So terrible."

"Yeah, I heard on the radio. I hope they find her soon."

"She used to walk from her house to play with the boys all the time. They live just back through the woods. Everyone is so worried the wolves got her."

Lakin paused, looking back into the trees. So many houses lay just within reach of the wilds of the forest here. Just a little patch of clearing where humans convinced themselves they were in civilization, when really they were just barely warding off ferality.

"Would it be alright, Mrs. Baldwin, if I walked the woods? Since there's worry about wolves... I wouldn't mind just checking it out. I won't be a bother for long. Just looking for signs."

Marie seemed unsure but eventually nodded with a smile. "Of course, Mr. Douglas. Anything to help."

iii.

The first time she tried to end her own life she claimed it was an accident, and he believed her. It wasn't until the doctor told him they'd pumped what equated to nearly thirty pills out of her stomach that he realized. Those little pills that were supposed to help her, make her feel better. He asked her why, from the side of the bed. He saw the black pits under her eyes, like she was becoming transparent to reveal the darkness beneath. She started crying, and he couldn't stand it. He would have done anything to never see her like that again.

She was changed somehow, from that point. She was thin and frail. Fragile like the wings of some rare, delicate moth. She sought out lonely places. Quiet, dark places.

And, finally, she slept and slept and slept.

eleven

Lakin never thought that he would grow weary of being in the forests. He never thought that it would start to fill him with some sort of unease and discontent like it did now. The woods behind the Baldwin property were littered with garbage: mostly old plastic bags, feed sacks, and beer cans. The farther he went into the forest, the cleaner it became. He found that there was a well-worn trail that cut through the woods and consisted of sandy substrate that he was sure would be soft on the feet of bare-soled children who decided to venture out.

He walked along the same trail that he was sure the missing girl had likely traveled, and it almost made him sick. Anything could have happened to her, walking through the woods alone like this. He had been traveling for five or ten minutes now, and although the path was not the least bit treacherous, it was isolated. Beast, or worse, man, could be lying in wait for the young girl. She could have wandered off the path and gotten injured, unable to return home...

He stopped briefly, putting a hand to his chest. He didn't want to think about it anymore. This wasn't his job, wasn't his concern. Why couldn't he stop worrying about it? He hated to admit that it was a morbid curiosity and a suspicion that there was something terrible, dark, and vile going on here in Rotten Fork. Something very human. He also didn't want to admit that he felt like Shaw was involved somehow.

It wasn't that he necessarily thought that Shaw was capable of killing a man, a kid, and bathing in the blood of goats and 4H cows by moonlight... but he certainly seemed suspicious. Somehow guilty, somehow hiding something, somehow trying to cover it all up. Things like this didn't just happen back to back, or maybe that was the wicked charm of a small town. You could literally get away with murder.

His eyes were drawn to something off the trail, maybe ten yards into the trees. It was something fluttering, pink, waving in the gentle breeze. He looked around as though he suspected that someone might be following him. Satisfied that he was still alone, Lakin began walking through the briars and brush to get to it.

As he approached, he realized it was a little plastic flag, like one you'd put on the back of a go-kart or bicycle to keep track of it. The fluorescent fabric made a crinkling noise in the wind and seemed to mark a small building.

The structure was only chest high on Lakin and was made out of what appeared to be old siding and other scrap materials. Faded paint on the outside showed what had once been a bright rainbow. This must have been a little fort, and he suspected it had belonged to Dulcie Lloyd.

Lakin was hesitant to go inside, thinking about the rumors that would begin if he were found in the missing girl's hideout... As an outsider, he imagined it would be easy to try to pin something on him, although he hoped Marie could offer him the excuse of having permission to look in the woods for signs of wolves.

He pushed the little door open, finding rolled-out, curled linoleum on the interior, laid directly against the naked forest floor. Good way to get a snake bite, he thought. Although most snakes would avoid human contact whenever possible, this was a tempting place for them to get up under the sun-warmed linoleum where it stretched underneath the walls of the fort, and kids were always heavy footed. There was a series of abandoned dirt dauber nests on the wall which were also painted in a series of rainbow colored stripes. Lakin smiled at them.

It was a good thing he'd brought gloves. He put them on before clambering down on his knees. He crawled into the small abode, looking at the little windchimes made of bones and metal pieces, bottle caps made into candles. There were chip bags in a waste bin in the corner and a plastic mirror tacked to the wall. A dishtowel, embroidered around the edges with small flowers, had been fashioned into a curtain in front of a crookedly cut window.

He found several other trinkets inside, but there was one in particular that caught his attention. It hung on a nail above the door, and he remembered hitting his head on it when he came inside. He had forgotten about it at first, being caught up in the quaint little interior, and having initially passed it off as another windchime or even a dense section of cobweb.

It was a little painted wooden thing hanging from a long red string. It had a round, fat body, and a little curl on top of its head. He thought, maybe, it was a bobwhite quail. It was a peculiar thing for a child to have and choose to hang above the door. The nail had been driven in by an adult, he was sure, and it was ringed by a rusted horseshoe.

Lakin crawled back out of the house, standing up and stretching his back. He had gotten something wet on his pants, he assumed stagnant water from leaf litter. He reached down and dusted it off the knees, finding that it was mucilaginous. He could feel the difference even through his gloved hands. He wiped the thickness on his thighs, looking down to see what looked like...

It was. It was blood. His knees were bloodstained, tacky with the drying fluid. He jerked his gloves off, throwing them down onto the ground as he stumbled backwards and sprinted back to the trail.

twelve

Lakin had been so panicked about the blood on his clothes that he had run back to the Baldwin house and gotten straight into his car. He had heard the screen door open just as his car door shut. In his rearview, he saw Marie standing on the porch with the door propped against her knee. Had she wanted to talk to him? Tell him goodbye? She probably wanted to know what he'd found, if anything, but Lakin didn't want her to see him with the blood on his clothes.

The cab was filled with a saccharine odor, the smell of something old-dead. Rotting. Decay. It was an animal, he thought. It could've been a dead animal. A bird that flew in and couldn't get out. A raccoon may have carried in some carrion and left a puddle of blood. No matter how many scenarios he came up with, something just felt wrong. Something felt ominous.

Just as he turned into the cabin's driveway, he realized in his horror that he had thrown down his bloody gloves, leaving them there in the forest. His gloves with the blood of...

God, he hoped it was the blood of some animal. Of anything other than that little girl. Should he get ahead of it and explain? Call Shaw and just tell him everything? He supposed that call would have to be prefaced with an apology...

"Dammit, dammit!" He slammed the vehicle into park so quickly that he nearly hit his head on the windshield. He was sweating now, and he bolted into the cabin, head swimming. The room spun around him, and he stumbled into the counter on his way to the bathroom. He vomited into the toilet (mostly; there were several stray chunks on the seat and on the floor). He took off his clothes and shoved them into a corner, flipping on the shower, only to find that there was no water.

The pipes groaned, filling the house with a skull-rattling moan. The toilet then struggled to flush. The springhouse. The damn springhouse. The pump was frozen over, just like Shaw told him it might end up. He had thought, with the weather warming, that he would be in the clear.

"Not now," he begged. "Not now."

He had never wanted to shower more than now. Although he had not gotten the blood on his hands, he felt like he was drenched in it. He thought he could feel it on his knees and his thighs, against his fingers. He quickly pulled on a pair of jogging pants and put a jacket over his bare skin.

He put his boots on, unlaced, and tramped clumsily down the steep decline behind the cabin. It was a dark and damp journey, like he was making a descent into night. He could even hear the gentle click and grumble of frogs and insects, and he thought it was just a little warmer than it had been at the higher elevation.

The springhouse loomed ahead like a witch's cottage: a simple building with a wooden door and open windows. It was made primarily of old stone but appeared to have one section of much more modern construct off to one side. As he approached, the hair on the back of his neck stood on end, and his skin seemed to pull tighter in bumpy sections.

Lakin knew something was dead and rotting inside the springhouse before he even entered. The scent emanated from the windows and the hanging wooden door. It was a poor design, he thought; animals could climb in and die, or worse, possibly contaminate the water supply. He could hear the pleasant bubbling water inside and the faint patter of droplets on stone.

He put his palms on the wooden door, but it would not budge. He shoved his shoulder against it next, door squeaking against the floor. That was when it pushed open just enough that he saw something there.

Not just anything, but a body.

He took a few steps back, voice shrill. "Are you alright in there?"

He knew they weren't. The smell made sense, now. He rammed his body against the door, forcing it open and leaving a bloody smear across the stone floor. The corpse had once been a man, best Lakin could tell. He was still covered in some frost, from the cool and damp of the building, although it had warmed up outside over the last few days. It made his brown coat and gray hair glitter with silver powder.

Lakin didn't bother checking for a pulse and didn't bother trying to fix the water. He started walking up to the cabin more slowly now, considering very carefully how to proceed from here. He was sick to his stomach, but not necessarily with the sight of the body... instead, he was horrified at how this looked.

He went to the bathroom first, taking his bloodstained pants from the corner and chucking them into the bathtub. He jerked the shower curtain closed, metal rings clattering across the bar as they hid away the evidence for him. He took several deep breaths before he grabbed his cell phone, holding the device in his shaking palms.

He reluctantly dialed Shaw's number, holding the phone up to his ear as he sank down onto the floor. Shaw answered quickly, too enthusiastic as always. How could you be so happy to get a call from a guy who decked you in the nose?

"Lakin, how are you?" Shaw said, voice light and friendly.

He struggled, catching himself before he called him 'Sheriff' or 'Mr. Lowell.' "Shaw, listen. I went down to the springhouse..."

"Ah, that pump freeze up on you? I thought maybe you'd dodged the bullet, since it had started warming up a little. We've got another cold front coming in, though, so best you get acquainted with it. Did you have any issues?"

Lakin rubbed the bridge of his nose, eyes closed. If Shaw hadn't interrupted him, he would know that Lakin did in fact have an issue. He would admit that the annoyance at Shaw's tendency to talk over him did take the edge off of the panic he had otherwise been fighting off.

"Yeah, there's... there's a body in there, Shaw."

There was silence on the other end of the line.

"Shaw, did you hear me? I need you to get out here, with an ambulance... or something."

"Well," Shaw said, sighing loudly into the receiver. "I don't think an ambulance is going to do anyone a lot of good if they're dead, Lakin. Me and a few of the deputies will be down in a few minutes. Don't go anywhere, okay?"

"Why would I go anywhere?"

"I'm hoping you don't have any reason to," Shaw said, voice very matter-of-fact. "I'm just making sure that you hear me tell you not to. Just sit tight; we'll be there in a half hour."

Lakin had thirty minutes to sit alone and think. Did he mention his journey into the woods behind Marie's? Something told him that he didn't need to tell Shaw anything that wasn't necessary. He didn't want to get caught in a lie, but he thought that perhaps the exclusion of certain things would be okay. This man was not on his side, and something suspicious was going on in this town.

Lakin wasn't sure that he wanted to be caught in the middle of it.

The police pulled up with their sirens off, lights off. Without any sense of urgency, they followed Lakin down to the springhouse at the bottom of the hill. Lakin tried not to look Shaw in the face, although the man seemed in good spirits, as always. One eye was bruised and the skin on his nose was cracked with a black scab and what could've been stitches. Lakin couldn't tell at a distance. He squeezed the hand that he'd used to punch him, feeling only the slightest tightness and ache where tiny vessels had ruptured under the skin.

The two other deputies stood back while Shaw stuck his head inside, shoving the door open so roughly that the stiff body toppled and then rolled across the floor and out of the way. Lakin stood back as well, hand over his mouth in case he became sick.

Shaw crouched down, slowly and tediously examining the body. Lakin caught the deputies looking over at him suspiciously before turning their gazes back to Shaw as he worked. They murmured between them, speaking so hushed that Lakin had no doubt it was their intent for him not to hear.

Shaw finally returned to them, first addressing the other cops.

"You boys call the coroner, have them come pick him up, and then get a report written up. We're going to say it was natural causes."

The two men nodded and started back up the hill, and Shaw approached Lakin.

"Well, Lakin," Shaw said, crossing his arms over his chest and shaking his head. He looked at the body inside the stone building.

"Well?" Lakin parroted quietly.

Suddenly, Shaw made a face, laughing. Lakin was startled, jumping at the sudden sound.

"Are those the same pants you were wearing when we found Tony?"

Lakin looked down awkwardly at the gray sweatpants. "I... I don't know."

"Those are the same damn pants. The same damn pants. Those your murder pants, Lakin? You wear those pants to murder people?" Shaw was grinning, eyebrows bouncing, as he teased him.

"I... well, you know I haven't hurt anyone, right? I don't even know that man. Who is he? How did he get down there?"

"I'm afraid that's Ivan Practchett, our groundskeeper, housekeeper, whatever. The guy who cleaned up around the cabin and took care of everything for us."

"You didn't know he was missing? He's been down there for... a while."

"Claire came to pay him, to make sure that he knew we didn't need him for the next several weeks. We knew you'd be coming up, and then after that is usually around the time I come and stay for a week or so to do some grouse hunting. When she came by, he wasn't there. She found his key, figured he'd gone home for the season and forgot his check."

It was Lakin's turn to be silent. He couldn't imagine that anyone in this area just 'forgot their check.' People relied on every dime they could scrape up in these small towns.

"So you went down to check the pump, huh?" Shaw asked.

"Yes, I got here and tried to take a shower... The water wouldn't run. So I walked down."

"Where had you been the earlier part of the day?"

Lakin shifted. "I went to the grocery store and then stopped to make sure Marie Baldwin was doing okay."

Shaw furrowed his brow and cocked his head, pulling his lower lip in between his teeth. "Marie Baldwin?"

"Yes, I just wanted to make sure she was holding up okay. It was a stressful situation. I took her kids some dessert from the store."

Shaw was looking at Lakin in a way that unnerved him.

"So Marie would confirm you were there, right?"

"Of... course. Why wouldn't she?"

"Guess it depends on why you were actually there."

"I don't understand," Lakin started. "I went there, and came..."

He swallowed. He was going to say that he came straight back here. If Shaw was actually suspicious about Lakin's whereabouts and questioned Marie she'd likely tell him about Lakin going up through the woods. They'd find the blood; they'd find his gloves. He nervously ran his fingers down his thumbs and up his palms at his sides.

"He probably had a heart attack. Wasn't the picture of health, you know. You've likely got nothing to worry about," Shaw said, patting Lakin on the back as he started up the hill.

"Hey, Shaw," Lakin called after him.

Shaw stopped, turning around and making a hum in his throat as though to ask what Lakin wanted.

"I'm sorry about..." He motioned around his face in a circle. "I don't know what got into me. I'm sorry."

"Not yet, you aren't," Shaw said with a broad smile, waving his hand in the air dismissively before he started back up the hill.

Lakin felt the color and warmth drain from his face and he took several steps up the hill. "What?"

"I said no problem, I know you are," Shaw called back, not turning around this time as he continued up the incline and out of sight.

thirteen

Lakin sat at the table with a hot cup of coffee on top of a folded napkin. He had worried that the cup might sweat in the cool air and leave a ring on the rustic surface. He needed to add some more wood to the stove, but the piles of stove lengths were starting to dwindle, and he didn't want to ask Shaw where more might be stashed. He also hesitated to touch the axe he had found outside, not without gloves. At this point he was avoiding anything that didn't belong to him and could be considered a weapon.

His laptop was open, and he had tried to run the internal email service for the lab, photos uploaded to send to his best friend there. He had known Tyler since college. They had attended the same school, roomed together, and then applied to the lab together. They had been a package deal for as long as either one could remember. Tyler was Lakin's best man at his wedding, and he was the first one, the only one, he called when Lena died.

He watched as the blue bar slowly crept across the screen, trying to gently push the email through to Tyler's address. While he waited, he grabbed his phone and dialed his number, gingerly sipping the still hot coffee.

"Lakin," Tyler's voice came across the line enthusiastically. "How are you, man?"

"It's really good to hear your voice," Lakin responded, voice exasperated.

"Are you alright? Sounding a little stressed..."

He could hear the obvious concern in Tyler's tone.

"It's just... there's a lot of really weird shit going on up here."

"What kind of weird shit?"

"Some guy killed himself, there's a girl missing, I found a dead guy in the springhouse behind the cabin I'm staying at."

"Holy fuck..." Tyler piped.

"The worst part is the sheriff has it out for me. I can't explain it, but he keeps making these jabs at me. Like he wants to blame me for what's going on."

"Get out of there. That sounds like a shitshow you don't need to get wrapped up in. What did they call us for anyway... nuisance animal, right?"

"Yeah, they think it's wolves."

Tyler scoffed, "Of course they do, and I'm sasquatch."

"Well... that's the thing, Tyler. I found them. I found the wolves."

A long pause, and then: "You're shitting me."

"I'm not. I haven't seen a lot of them, but at least one family group, which makes me feel confident there's a decent population here. I don't know how they've been here without anyone at the lab knowing, but..."

"Rufus, you think?" Tyler asked, calling the red wolf by its Latin name.

"I don't know. Either some subspecies or maybe even a hybrid. I'm sending you photos and some other info... or trying. The internet isn't very reliable."

"So you got enough proof just come back home, and we'll set up a study plan and proposal and..."

"Yeah, I know I need to get out. I just... I'm kind of invested in what's going on. I know I don't usually get caught up in proving someone wrong but ... I really want to be able to throw it in this sheriff's face."

"You aren't the Hardy Boy type. So something's got you interested... Tell me what it is."

"The sheriff wants me to blame all of the deaths and attacks on wolves. When he called me up here of course it was just animal attacks, but I keep finding... This is going to sound crazy. I keep finding human footprints, where all the animals are dead. And I found a missing dog's head stacked on top of a goat's head on a fencepost. Tell me an animal did that."

"Doesn't he believe you? What do you think is going on?"

"I don't know... all I know is he's up to something."

"The sheriff?"

"Yeah. He's a really shady character."

"Well, as soon as the email comes through, I can put together the study report for you, if you want. Then maybe I can get a team together and we can come up and keep you company. At least you wouldn't be so... isolated."

"Yeah, I'd like that... I'm a little uncomfortable. I feel trapped."

"Where are you staying?"

"The sheriff has a hunting cabin, it's right off the highway, though. Not too secluded."

"Just be careful. That sounds like the kind of thing you watch in movies."

"I know. It seems unreal. I keep thinking that maybe I'm misreading him, the sheriff. I don't know. Anyway, these files look like they're finally attached, so I'm going to send them on over. I'll try to keep you updated."

"That's great. I'll start on it as soon as I can. Hey, Lakin. How are you?" Tyler emphasized the word so he could ask about the grief without giving it a name.

Lakin shrugged one shoulder, slumping back into the chair as he briefly looked up at the cabin's ceiling. How was he? He didn't know how to even answer that question. He didn't know how much to tell Tyler and how much to omit.

"I'm okay. I still have dreams about her... those nightmares. But I think, and I can't believe I'm saying this, I think being up here has helped. I'm too worried about getting murdered in my sleep to dwell on the past too much."

"Okay, man," Tyler whispered. "Just let us know if you need us, we're here for you. Okay? All of us."

"I know you are. I know."

"Alright, we'll talk soon."

They said their goodbyes, and then Lakin hung up, making sure the email was successfully sent before he closed the program. When the search engine showed up, blank and ready to answer his questions, he paused. First, he searched: 'Lowell Rotten Fork.'

He found a few search results, mostly from outdated websites that detailed the history of the small town. It was some information he had already come across while investigating the history of the town's unique name. The pages were poorly laid out, walls and walls of text with off-set photos and plenty of grammatical errors. He decided to save himself some time and ctrl+f on the first page of history, searching for 'Lowell,' specifically. It found ten instances of the word.

Rotten Fork was settled in 1823 and was initially densely occupied by saltpeter and coal mines. The Lowell* family was gifted the deed to the young town under unusual circumstances when Saindon Lowell (née Lewellen) rescued then town leadership official, Lewis Davidtz, from a collapsed mine. This was a topic of hot debate for many years, as just after he signed over the deed and his worldly possessions, he succumbed to his injuries.

*The Lowells immigrated as and were previously known as the Lewellen family. For genealogy purposes, please research by this name as well. When the family settled into the Wolf Valley where The Gray River is birthed, they were given the name Lowell instead: which translates roughly to 'the young wolves.'

"Well, good to know that the Lowell family has been sketchy since the beginning of time..." Lakin muttered to himself. "At least Shaw comes by it honest."

He clicked through to the next instances of the name, finding two other sections where the remaining six were found. Nothing of any real interest, so he moved on to the next results on the search engine. He found information about both Shaw and his father being law enforcement officers in the county. He found an article about Shaw and Claire getting married, with a grainy photo of them cutting a small cake in an outdoor wedding surrounded by people of the town. Something about it felt intrusive, and Lakin quickly clicked off of it.

He did another search, this time for 'wolves Rotten Fork,' which generated little more than cryptozoology sites, speculation, hunters claiming they had seen the wolves. Then he came upon something he wished he wouldn't have.

LOCAL MYTHS AND LEGENDS
By Simon Boyd

Rotten Fork, like many towns in our region, is rich with local folklore. One of the most fascinating and ancient myths is that of the midlem, which is a colloquial term for 'middlemen' or spirits that take the form of an animal to guide souls to the afterlife. In Rotten Fork, the myth goes deeper. It is said that in a secret and inaccessible forest in the valley, there is a temple where something even more terrifying is born: lycanthropes. Locals would like to pretend that the Fork is not riddled with dark history: murders, disappearances, and other tragedies all centralizing around this one forbidden forest. For the skeptics, some explanations for the strange behaviors and belief that they have transformed when entering the forest have stemmed from invasive fungal spores from native mushrooms, noxious gasses from organic decomposition in the swamps, and natural magnetic or electrical disturbances.

Lakin didn't believe in nonsense like werewolves and spirit guides, but he did believe in mania and delirium. There were plenty of instances when people, entire communities, believed in something that had a perfectly natural explanation. If this forest was real, and locals believed that it was... what, possessed? Haunted? Cursed? If he could find it, it might hold some sort of clue as to what was going on here. He could drop some hints to Shaw about it and see if it was something he believed in or, worse, embellished.

He had a plan and was about to close the article when he noticed something else. The article was authored by Simon Boyd. It took him several moments to realize why the name had any significance to him.

The Boyd house; where he had found the wolves. Could this be the same Boyds? He decided that he would call Chitto first, to ask him about the forest and the property.

Most importantly, though, to ask what happened to their daughter before they left town.

fourteen

"I'll swing by and pick you up," Chitto had said.

It was something he could get used to about the little town. He called Chitto to see if he had time to answer a few questions, and then in the next breath Chitto was offering to get him so they could talk in person.

The beat-up Jeep with the noisy exhaust and rattling frame pulled up outside. Lakin heard it coming long before he heard it idle, and a ping came across his phone with a text from Chitto announcing his arrival. Lakin almost sprinted out the door, locking it carefully behind him before he walked through the muck to the Jeep. The door squeaked as he opened it and then made a grinding sound when it closed. Inside, Lakin swore he could see the road through a half-dollar-size hole in the floor, and everything, including Lakin's ass, shook as they took off down the road.

"So you had some stuff you wanted to talk about?" Chitto asked. Lakin was surprised that he cut straight to the chase, but he could see the immense curiosity on his face. He thought it was probably one of two things: Chitto wanted to be helpful, or he craved all of the gossip (if there was any).

Lakin nodded, rubbing his bare hands together, prefacing: "This is going to make me sound like I'm crazy."

"No pressure, I already think you are," he laughed.

"First, I've got to tell you something. I've got to tell somebody, so that somebody knows. I took Marie and her kids some dessert yesterday, just to be friendly, you know? To make sure she was doing alright. I walked up through the woods behind her place, and found a fort."

"A fort?" Chitto seemed puzzled.

"Like... like a kid's play fort. It was that missing girl's."

"Dulcie Lloyd."

"Yeah. I went into the fort just to look around. Curious, you know. Found some weird stuff. There was a horseshoe above the door and a little wooden bird. It had a little curly thing on its head like a bobwhite. Any idea what that's all about?"

"Well, sounds like someone was trying to protect her. Those would be things you'd hang on a doorway or above the window. Quail, specifically, in like a kid's room or something."

"Weird..." Lakin whispered quietly, then apologized in a louder tone. "Sorry. Just... for some reason that gives me the creeps."

"Her parents don't seem the type for folk magic. Mostly older people in the area, and for the most part it's tinctures and herbal treatments, planting by moon phases, and stuff like that. You'll dig up a protection jar here and there, but yeah. I could see why you'd think it was odd to find that stuff in a kid's playhouse."

"And while I was there, I found blood."

The Jeep veered over the rumble strip before Chitto corrected it. "What?"

"It was on my pants when I got out and then on my gloves. I dropped my gloves there."

"Jesus Christ, Lakin. Did you tell Shaw?"

"No... I can't tell him."

"You need to tell him before their investigation takes them up there and they find your bloody gloves... Do you know how bad that looks? You're some outsider that no one knows, and there's a missing girl. Maybe a dead girl... if it was her blood."

"Listen, I came straight to the cabin when I saw the blood. I was scared. Got there and found the body of the groundskeeper in the pumphouse."

"Ivan?"

"Yeah. Shaw was making weird comments about me murdering people and showing up at these crime scenes. I couldn't... I couldn't tell him that I'd also found evidence that the little girl's hurt or dead..."

"Okay, okay... Maybe we can get out there and get the gloves. I don't want to be involved in all of this, but.. You get into any more trouble, though, and I'm not going to be able to help you out. Alright?"

"Yeah... Did you know that Shaw's family basically owned Rotten Fork for a while?"

"Yeah, just a little local history."

"Did you know his last name means 'young wolf'?"

"No... What does your last name mean?"

"I don't know..."

"Probably means 'paranoid conspiracy theorist', but I don't think that necessarily signifies anything..." Chitto snarked.

"Okay... Can you tell me what happened with the Boyds?"

Chitto looked at him out of the corner of his eye, almost as though he was nervous about the question that had been presented. He cleared his throat, alternating the hand he was using to steer the rusty vehicle along the Fork's backroads.

"What's going on, Lakin? What's with all these weird questions?"

"I'm just trying to piece together some things," Lakin responded awkwardly.

"If you're trying to involve Shaw in some kind of weird scenario, I want no part in it. I do not want to get involved in a mess like that or give him any reason to come after me."

"Why is everyone afraid of him?"

"What are you talking about? I'm not afraid of Shaw... who's afraid of Shaw?"

"Nevermind, so can I ask you about the Boyds? Just pretend I'm a curious tourist."

"Sure, what do you want to know about them?"

"You said there was an accident... with their daughter," Lakin started gingerly.

"Jesus Christ..." Chitto whispered.

"I'm just trying to piece some things together, that's all. I read some articles online written by Simon Boyd. It seemed like he was really interested in the area. I was just wondering what happened to make them pack up and move."

"Simon was apparently big into local folklore and spent a lot of time looking for something in the locust forest."

"Locust forest?" Lakin interjected.

"There's a honey locust grove, near the Boyd place. Lots of weird rumors and myths surrounding it. Majority of it is pretty swampy."

"Yeah, in the article I read, Simon Boyd mentioned that a lot of things have happened there and that people tried to blame it on something natural... but he seemed to think it was something supernatural."

Chitto nodded. "Yeah, he sure did. He bought into the urban legends and obsessed over it. Nothing weird has ever happened there that I know of, I mean, nothing real. Nothing confirmed, for sure. Aside from the occasional drunk teenagers getting hurt tromping around there at night or something. Nothing except the one incident."

"What incident?" he coaxed.

"Well, that's just it. Simon was out there one day, messing around with shit he doesn't understand. His daughter followed him; he'd gone on foot. She snuck out while her mom was taking a nap and went out there. Nobody really knows what happened, but she had some kind of episode. Simon had to carry her back home and call an ambulance. He went a little crazy, had this big story about the forest doing it to her, that she'd touched something. But he was off his rocker. They moved away after a little while. Went somewhere where they could more easily care for her, I think."

"Where's the forest?"

"You don't need to go looking around there, Lakin. You're spooked. Someone with the mindset you've got right now doesn't need to go into a place where there's all that... myth status."

"You don't believe in it?"

Chitto shrugged, flipping on a turn signal as he slowed to a stop sign, although Lakin was sure the blinking light didn't work.

"I don't know. I think some places have bad energy, you know? Bad things that have happened and compounded. Sometimes you shouldn't go messing with that kind of thing, even if you don't believe in the place itself being evil or... whatever. I just don't like to tempt that kind of thing myself."

"Where are we going?" Lakin finally asked as the car rolled down an unfamiliar road.

"I'm going to see Holly about a horse."

"Holly Grant?"

"Gernt. Yeah, she is a horse broker. The ex-wife says our daughter has got the horse bug, so I'm going to see what she's got. Figured you could tag along and we could have these weird conversations about the boogeyman in the woods and chupacabra and shit on the way."

"Sorry, I'm not usually like this. I don't usually buy into these things."

"Why now?"

Lakin shook his head, not responding. He didn't really know.

They pulled down a long dirt driveway that was surprisingly dry, considering the recent thaw. Lakin wondered if they were using something for drainage, like crusher run or larger stones. The drive was in better shape than most of the highways in the town.

The Jeep rolled to a park and a woman came out into the yard, waving wildly at them.

Holly was lively, bright. She had too much hair for her head. It was a curly mess of soft, glistening copper that seemed to be animated on its own. She had a freckled face that boasted no makeup, with a broad smile of charmingly imperfect teeth. There was something about her that made you happy instantly, warming you from your core like a shot of some strong drink. Lakin didn't fault Shaw for his attraction to her.

She greeted Chitto with a hug, which he accepted enthusiastically. He turned to introduce her to Lakin, who smiled and raised a hand in greeting.

"Lakin, this is Holly. Holly, this is Lakin Douglas. He's here about our wolf situation that he thinks isn't a wolf situation. I think I've mentioned him to you."

She looked him up and down, like she was sizing him up. "Nice to meet you, Lakin."

She offered a hand, which he shook. The moment he clasped his fingers around her rough palm, she pulled him into a tight embrace like she had known him her entire life.

"Welcome to Rotten Fork," she said as she pulled away. "And welcome to my humble farm. You'll be happy to know it's aptly named Wolf Ridge Ranch. On account of... you know, the imaginary wolves."

He sighed, "I deserve that."

Chitto slapped him on the back, "We're just teasing you. So, Holly, let's see what you got for my baby girl. I want something with three legs in the grave, alright?"

She laughed, slapping the dusty thigh of her blue jeans like he'd said something hilarious before she spun and started walking towards the barn. "Well, I don't have anything like that... but I do have a few that are more 'whoa' than 'go.' No push-button ponies or deadheads, but safe, sane, and sound? Sure."

Lakin followed them into the barn, where a few horses were stabled and waiting. Beyond the back door he could see other horses grazing in fields beyond. He guessed that these were the ones that she thought were suitable for Chitto's child. The smell of horses had always been pleasant to Lakin: sweetness, leather, hay, and animal sweat. He remembered taking Lena riding with him and Tyler once as they tracked game in the mountains. He had watched as she put her lips against the horse's velvet muzzle, breathing in its scent like some people inhale a cup of warm coffee. He had thought she glowed briefly when she exhaled, and it had made him fall in love all over again.

As Chitto and Holly went down to the stall on the opposite side, Lakin stopped to pet a bay gelding by the front doors. When he made sure they weren't looking, he cupped his hands around the horse's chin and sniffed its sweet-smelling nose with his eyes closed, reminiscing.

fifteen

He was lost in the swirling of the clothes in the front-facing washer, the gentle hum of the dryers that filled the laundromat, the aroma of dryer sheets and washing powder. The sudsy twirling of his clothes, his bloody clothes, had him somewhere far away. He wasn't sure he had blinked at all while he traveled there in his head. Went somewhere else. Somewhere even colder, even lonelier, even quieter, even more hostile.

His phone vibrated in his pocket against his leg, and it sent a shockwave through his body that was almost painful. He scrambled to pull the thing out of his pocket like it was hot. A short, elderly woman across the room was folding her towels, facing him, and her face was full of suspicion. She pushed her heavy, gold-framed glasses up onto her nose as she unashamedly watched every move he made.

His fumbling fingers nearly made him miss the call entirely, but he finally got it swiped to answer and put it to his ear.

"Yeah, hello?"

"Lakin." It was Chitto's voice. "You alright? You sound out of breath."

"Yeah, I'm just... I'm doing laundry."

"Oh...kay... Listen, I've got some bad news..."

Lakin listened as it sounded like Chitto was shifting around, and the sound of metal clanging suggested that he might have been getting into his Jeep.

"I went up to Marie's to find an excuse to walk back through the woods."

Lakin put his face in his hands, gut wrenching. He already knew what he was going to say. Shaw had found the gloves.

"Shaw was walking the trails between her house and the Lloyds' place. He had deputies with him, and some of the volunteer dogs. I don't think they found anything really significant, like no body or anything... but I just wanted to let you know. They did have evidence bags, so they've got something."

"He'll know they're mine. If he did find them, he will know they're mine."

"Maybe not..."

"They're these stupid fishing gloves we all found and wore. Everyone at the lab. He'll know. I've had them on around him."

"Okay, just try not to freak out. We'll come up with something. He has no reason to ask you about them."

"I had no reason to be up there, either."

"Yeah, but it's a little late to consider that now."

"Let me call you back."

"Alright," Chitto said, and they both hung up.

Lakin prematurely stopped the rinse cycle, quickly throwing the clothes into the nearest free dryer. When he turned around, the old woman was standing so close that his elbow brushed her soft breasts. He jerked his arm back to his body like it had offended him.

"Oh, I am so sorry, ma'am," he said, putting his palms up as he stepped backwards, backside bumping against the shaking dryer.

She was clutching a small, pleather handbag to her chest, and she reached down with a shaking hand to open it and start sifting through the contents. Finally, she pulled out a pamphlet, which she handed to him with those same quivering fingertips. Lakin took it from her gingerly, turning it around to see that it was for a group called Operation Sobriety. He smiled at her apologetically.

"Oh... No, ma'am... I don't have a drug problem," he stammered.

"Get down here so I can pray for you," she demanded, jerking on his arm roughly. Lakin dropped to his knee as commanded, tipping his head down and closing his eyes as she put one hand on the back of his head and one hand in the air and begged God to save his soul from his demons, right there in the middle of the LaundroMatic.

Lakin pulled into the cabin's slanted drive, jerking the car into park more harshly than he intended. He noticed something wasn't right. The cabin's door was ajar, gently moving in and out with the breeze. When he was outside of the vehicle, he held the button for the handle and pushed the car door closed to soften the sound of the latch before he started walking towards the door with caution in his step.

He was surprised to see Claire Lowell standing inside the cabin, almost as surprised as she appeared to be to see him there. She spun around, her hair flitting around her shoulders in wisps as she fixed on him a startled glare.

She put a hand to her chest, smiling. "Oh, Mr. Douglas. You scared me."

"Mrs. Lowell," Lakin said quietly, hovering in the doorway. "What..."

He wanted to ask what are you doing here? Which was the most accurate and appropriate question, but he reminded himself that this was her property, although he was staying there.

"How can I help you?" he instead asked. "Do you need something?"

"Oh, no," she said, moving across the floor towards him, stopping to rest with her hands on the back of the chair. "I was just stopping in to look for a set of spare keys that our groundskeeper had. He usually kept them tucked away in here somewhere."

Lakin wondered why he would have a set of spare keys to the cabin in the cabin. Don't flatter yourself; why else would she be here?

"I can give you more time to look. I was just in town doing laundry. I have a few more things I need to do, anyway." He motioned back out the door.

"No, no. That's fine. I don't need them that bad. Shaw just likes things like that accounted for, you know. Something scary about someone having a key to a place you sleep, you know."

"Yeah," he agreed.

"Come on in, you're letting the chill in."

"Oh, that's okay," he said nervously. What if Shaw drove by on his way from Marie's and saw her car here? He'd… Lakin looked over his shoulder, quickly noting there was no other car here. Of course, he would've noticed it when he pulled up.

"How did you get here?" he added.

"Oh, I walked. Through the woods. I like a little hike now and again. Clear my thoughts, get some peace and quiet." She continued to smile at him, and, Christ, she was beautiful.

He hesitantly walked inside, waiting for her to move away from the chair so he could easily pass through, but instead she stood there, forcing him toe-to-toe with her as he turned his face away and slid into the kitchen.

"Can I make you some coffee?" he asked.

"That would be lovely," she said, seating herself at the table. "I heard that you and my husband had an altercation when Tony was found."

As she said this, Lakin's hand began to shake. He passed it off as intentional, shaking more noticeably to deposit the scoops of coffee into the filter.

"It was a misunderstanding," Lakin said quietly.

"It sounded more unprovoked to me."

Lakin didn't turn around to look at her as he listened to the coffee pot gurgle and deposit a sweet smelling stream of liquid into the glass. There was a sudden thickness to the air, a heaviness that he felt at his back. He thought that if he turned around, she would be standing there, breathing against the back of his neck. Why did he feel so intimidated by her?

"I'm sure he felt that way," Lakin agreed. "I apologized to him later, I just misinterpreted something he said."

She hmm'd in her throat, a vague response, as he set a mug in front of her and seated himself two chairs away at the table. She hesitantly sipped her hot coffee, testing the temperature before she attempted a longer swallow. She didn't respond to him directly, but her eyes never left his.

"I've been meaning to talk to Shaw, actually... but maybe you could help me with some information instead," he suggested. He wasn't actually going to talk to Shaw about this, and he was sure that Claire would relay the information to her husband, but at least it would give him a head start.

"What kind of information?"

"Do you know where the locust forest is? Somewhere behind the Boyd place?"

Her interest was piqued, her soft features hardening somewhat, eyes narrowing in suspicion. She set the steaming cup down in front of her.

"Why do you ask?"

"Saw some pictures of the trees online and they looked like really extreme specimens," he lied. "I wanted to see it for myself, maybe take some pods to the lab."

"There are pictures online?"

"Oh, yeah. There's pictures of everything online."

"That forest is very... special to a lot of people in this area. Older people, people who have been in this area for a long time. It's an unspoken rule that you don't tell people where it is, and no one respectable would take photos of it..."

Lakin faltered for a moment, stammering that maybe the trees were of a different grove.

"Who told you where it was?" she went on, leaning towards him.

"No one... I just..."

"Was it Chitto?"

"No... I saw an article... an old article from Simon Boyd. Online. The way he wrote about it, I just assumed it had to be close to his property. Otherwise how would he have stumbled upon it?"

Claire looked suspicious, but she sat back in her seat and took another sip of coffee.

"I'm sorry if I upset you. I really meant no disrespect."

Claire waved her hand dismissively. "Just don't get tangled up in things you don't understand, Lakin."

"It could be beneficial to my research, was all that I was thinking. I am inclined to be curious."

"Do you know what they say about cats?"

He thought he caught a glimpse of something threatening in her eyes, but it was replaced with a playful twinkle as she offered a crooked smile.

"What do you know about the place, then? I read that Simon's daughter had an accident or something. A lot of

people believe it has some kind of bad energy or something...
something supernatural?"

"I never liked that word..." she admitted. "Super
natural. Sometimes these things that we don't understand are
the most natural things, older than what we know of as nature.
Things we want to admit and understand as nature."

"So you believe it, then."

"I believe that there is something ancient there,
something that doesn't need to be poked and prodded and
studied. Something that will not tolerate that sort of intrusion.
I think if you go there with no respect, you'll get the same
treatment anyone would if you walked into their domain with
that kind of indignant nature."

"I'm surprised."

"Oh?" she laughed, smiling at him. "Why is that?"

"I thought your family wasn't from this area. You
sound like a native of Rotten Fork. A Rotten Forkian? A
Forker?"

She shrugged, smile unfaltering. "Maybe my experience
with that place was a little different than other trespassers'.
Sometimes when you go in knowing what you want, what you
need, you receive it."

There was a grumble on the road and Lakin cleared his
throat, forcing his eyes away from her to watch as a car drove
by. It was Shaw's vehicle. He tried not to look back at her too

quickly; he could see her staring a hole through him in his peripheral vision. His heart skipped a beat as the vehicle slowed by the driveway, not quite stopping, and then it turned into the drive.

He took a steady inhale and a slow blink before turning back to her.

But she wasn't there.

iv.

She had good days in between.

Ephemeral contentment.

Transient happiness that they both clutched at until they smothered it in their desperation to feel, love, and experience every fugitive second.

sixteen

Shaw had entered the cabin like he... well, like he owned the place. Which, Lakin reminded himself, he did. He seemed to be looking for something when he came in, brow furrowed as he turned and glanced around as though something was out of place. He took the hat off of his head and patted it against his thighs.

"Are you... looking for something?" Lakin asked, keeping his voice low and polite.

"I just..." Shaw spun around slowly before noticing the empty coffee cup still sitting where Claire had been. Then he looked at the cup that Lakin had been using.

Lakin picked up the cup, hurrying to the sink with it. "Sorry, I'm being lazy. I left that there from last night. I couldn't sleep."

"Well, word from the wise... drinking coffee in the middle of the night isn't going to help you. Have you had a visitor recently?"

"Visitor?" Lakin asked, trying to sound casual and curious. "No... Nobody recently. I mean... Chitto was here a day or two ago, but he didn't come inside. Why do you ask?"

"There's just this... scent in the air. You know? Like a woman's perfume."

Lakin walked back over to the table, watching as Shaw made a wafting motion with his hand and inhaled. He motioned to Lakin, and he did the same thing but shrugged.

"I'm sorry, I don't smell anything, and I haven't had a female guest," Lakin said with a shrug, smiling appeasingly. "Was there something you stopped to talk to me about?"

"Actually, there was." Shaw pulled out the chair at the table, and Lakin followed his lead. Shaw laid his hat on the table, leaning on his elbows as he faced Lakin. His face twisted into an apologetic pucker, but his eyes seemed humored and mischievous.

"I really hate to do this to you, Lakin. I do."

Lakin's gut sank, and he sat back in his chair. "Do what?"

"I need to know where you were the morning that Tony Baldwin died. I know you were here when Marie started wandering down the road... but I'm going to need you to kind of... detail your day up until that point." Shaw retrieved a pen and pad of paper from his pocket, poising the utensil over the paper expectantly.

"I was... I was here, Shaw. I got straight out of bed and immediately saw her walking down the road."

"So you just so happened to wake up as she was passing by the house, is that what you're saying?"

"Yeah... there was a cat. I had let this cat inside, and it must've seen her because it wanted outside. When I opened the door, I saw her stumbling down the road. I was asleep before that and here the night before. You don't think I had anything to do with Tony, do you?"

"No," Shaw said with a laugh. "No. We ruled Tony's death an accident. Medical examiner said it could've been an animal attack. We never found anything in the way of ballistics evidence. Of course, we didn't tell Marie that."

"Then..." Lakin trailed off, shrugging, searching Shaw's face for answers.

Shaw sighed, laying the paper and pen down. He muttered Lakin's name a couple of times, like a parent chiding a disobedient child. He reached into his jacket pocket and pulled out Lakin's gloves, setting them on the tabletop between them.

Lakin stared at the gloves. He knew this was coming. Shaw seemed to be giving him time to think, sitting quietly in his chair. Lakin knew that he needed to just come clean. He needed to tell Shaw the truth. In the movies, people always tried to cover up what had happened because the circumstances were too strange. It always made them look more guilty. He needed to just be honest. The more he tried to hide this, the more it was going to look like he had something to do with it. He was the outsider, the stranger who had come into town with a tragic history. The disturbed loner. And now it only made sense that he, what... murdered a kid?

"Okay, I'm going to explain all of this to you," Lakin said calmly. He was surprised at how composed and collected he sounded.

"Oh, I hope so," Shaw said. "Don't tell me the cat that told you about Marie Baldwin took them out there, though. I'm not going to buy that."

"I went to Marie Baldwin's. Took her kids something to eat, just as a good gesture. Make sure they were alright. I think maybe I'd already told you that. She mentioned that the little girl who's missing used to walk between her house and their house, through the woods, and that there was a trail. I asked if I could walk the trail to look for signs of wolves. She told me some people were worried that wolves got her. I found a kids' playhouse or fort out there, and I dropped my gloves."

"There's blood on your gloves, Lakin."

"I didn't know it was blood," Lakin insisted "I thought maybe... but then I came home to wash my clothes because I panicked. I was going to call the police... call you. But that was when I found the groundskeeper in the pumphouse. Honest to

God, I didn't see anything else. I didn't do anything. I just went to the fort, looking for tracks and scat, and dropped my gloves."

"You didn't think to tell me, while I was here that day, that you might have found blood in a missing girl's fort?"

Lakin shook his head. "I was scared, Shaw. I've never been in the middle of something like this."

"You're in the middle of a lot of things right now... and at this point, you have interfered with an investigation."

He didn't respond, just stared. "Do I need to come and make an official statement or something? Do I need a lawyer?"

Shaw laughed, tucking the gloves back into his pocket. It was somewhat comforting; Lakin suspected that if they were going to be used as real evidence, they'd need to be in a bag or something. But instead they were naked inside the sheriff's pocket, flecks of dried blood flaking into the folds of fabric.

"Nah, not yet. We have dogs up there now, volunteers. If we find anything, I may need to ask you a few more questions. For now, why don't you just try to stay out of trouble and away from crimes, alright?"

"Yeah," Lakin whispered.

"Now that we got all of that serious business out of the way," he said in a mocking tone, like it was something he was forced to talk about before they could sit back and drink a beer together, "I heard you went up to Holly's place this week."

"Yeah.. Went out there on..."

"Making the rounds with the ladies, aren't you?"

"I just went up there with Chitto. He bought his daughter a horse."

"Holly said you were a really nice guy but kind of quiet. Mysterious, she said. I think she might like you."

Lakin watched Shaw's expression challenge him to engage, but he didn't. He remembered Chitto saying that Shaw and Holly had a thing, and he wasn't sure if that was ongoing or not. Was he jealous?

Lakin shrugged. "I barely talked to her. Chitto found what he wanted and we left."

"You're doing a lot of socializing for someone who's here to tell us about our animal problem. Are you ready to write up that report about the wolves? Can we say it was the wolves, yet?"

Lakin shook his head. "No. I don't think it was the wolves."

"I was afraid you'd say that," Shaw sighed. "It just doesn't make much sense, Lakin. This is a mighty strange hill to die on, but we have to stand by our decisions, don't we? Accept those consequences."

Shaw stood, dusting off his hat before he put it back on his head.

"I'll get to the bottom of this, I promise," Lakin assured him, offering his hand. Shaw looked down at it and laughed, and then he left.

seventeen

Another night of fitful sleep.

Lakin was in between; his mind was still churning, but his body was paralyzed in a semi-slumber. The cabin became eerily silent, even the copasetic static of his ears hushed. Then, he heard a creak. The floorboard in the center of the cabin made that exact sound: a groaning as weight was pressed upon it, then a gentle and high-pitched rumble as the weight was released. It was the precise sound; he knew it was.

He was too afraid that maybe he was dreaming again. He was afraid he'd see her: Lena, in those moments after her death. He swallowed, and the nausea felt tangible, real, and legitimate. It was then that he heard a gentle swishing, like the sound of her silk gown against the stubble of her legs, a shuffle of feet across the wood floor.

Then, Lakin felt the bed depress beside him, the way it used to when she would crawl across the bed to lie with him. He pursed his lips together, clenching his eyes closed so tightly that he saw bursts of stars behind them. His heart was making slow, forceful pounding in his chest. The bed sheet fluttered, cold air breezing underneath, but he was sweating. His damp skin chilled, gooseflesh covering his body. It was real.

"Please," he whispered quietly into the dark, eyes still clamped shut. "Just let me rest tonight."

The sensation of her cold toes against the back of his thigh, sliding down and across his calf, was too much. Lakin launched himself out of the bed, stumbling backwards away from the empty bed. Sheets still fluttered, but fell flush against the mattress. There was no one there.

He was panting, covered in perspiration... but now he could hear the ambience of night, the hum of his ears. He slowly reapproached the bed, ensuring that it was, in fact, vacant... and then he crawled back into it warily.

He pulled the sheets up in handfuls around his face, inhaling deeply as he sobbed. He could smell the faint aroma of her lotion on the fabric.

The next morning Lakin woke up like he was suffering from a hangover. His head was throbbing and his body ached. He clutched his pillow between his arms, and his shoulders were stiff and uncomfortable in their sockets. Even his jaw, from gritting his teeth all night, protested when he yawned.

It was cold inside the cabin. That was the first thing he noticed beyond his body's discomfort. At some point during the night, the smoldering embers of the fire had gone out, and there was a draft that chilled him to the bone. He had no intention of staying there any longer than it took to get ready, so he got to his feet and went to unpack clothes for the day.

The bag he was living out of was sitting open mouthed on the couch, and as he walked across the floor, he stepped in something wet and cold. He retreated a step, looking down to see a trail of water from the front door, across the floor, to the foot of the bed. No doubt, melted snow, but from where? Lakin's hair was standing on end. He knew better than this. He didn't believe in ghosts, spirits.

He forewent his shower, slipping on his clothes and boots, and went outside to look for any sign of life in the fresh snow. There were distinct imprints outside of the door: large enough to have been human footprints, but by now they were rising with the falling powder. Additional tracks circled down the side of the cabin,along the pathway hidden beneath the snow. By now, he couldn't tell how large the prints were, or if they were indeed shoes. He followed hesitantly, hoping he might find signs of a vehicle.

Instead, he found a dark stain in the snow. It was a blemish that was quickly disappearing beneath pure white, and Lakin snapped a twig off of a nearby tree to dig through the

fluff to uncover it. He jammed the stick into the now
uncovered shoe, lifting it up to examine it.

It was small enough to fit on his hand, pink with
patchy sequin pattering. It was covered in blood. Red coated
the interior of the shoe and the white laces, crusting around the
remaining gems. Lakin had no doubt that it was Dulcie
Lloyd's. Now he was confident that someone had been here.

He dropped the child's shoe back into the snow and
turned in a slow circle to try and catch sight of anyone who
might have been hiding in the treeline. No one was there; no
one that he could see, anyway. He left the shoe where it had
fallen and headed back up the trail to his parked truck. He
started the vehicle, which groaned in protest, and cranked on
the heat, despite how much he hated that dry air from the
vents. He felt so cold; an unearthly chill.

He drove with dedication to the Boyd place, leaning
over the steering wheel as he coasted down the highway. He had
only been there the single time, and it had been on foot from
Chitto's house through the woods. But he had seen the
highway when he found the corpse on the fenceline. He knew
it had to be here, somewhere.

He was surprised when he passed by Holly Gernt's on
the way, briefly disoriented. He hadn't realized how close
together all of these houses lay when they seemed, somehow, so
isolated. Her truck was sitting in the driveway near the

mailbox, door standing open. He slowed down, but when he saw her standing in the field, she raised a hand and he returned the gesture.

He was a little paranoid that she might call Shaw and ask what the out-of-towner was doing driving down this way. He hoped that if she was going to tell anyone, it would be Chitto, who, although he would be disappointed, would not meddle. He'd let Lakin get himself into trouble and expect him to get himself out of it. He finally saw the dilapidated fence and overgrown driveway of the Boyd's home, and he pulled down the road.

The driveway was unkempt and muddy from the melted snow. He briefly shifted the truck to low gear, having to ride crookedly on the embankment so the tires wouldn't fall into the deep ruts.

His heart sank as he approached the old home: absent of doors and windows, open and bare and exposed. There was a vehicle parked out front: a blue truck that was older but well maintained. He didn't recognize it as belonging to anyone familiar.

"Of course," he grumbled, shifting gears sloppily as his own vehicle finally plateaued onto the level ground of the old circle driveway. Of course someone would be there the day that he chose to try and snoop. His only hope was to turn around and pray they didn't see him... or he could go ahead and face them, tell them he wanted to have a look around. Geography. Mapping.

He reluctantly put the vehicle in park, exiting with as much confidence as he could muster. He left his gun in the back, phone in the passenger seat. The former intentional, the latter accidental.

"Hello?" Lakin called, baritone voice carrying through the quiet landscape.

"Hello," a voice, higher pitched and lower in volume, responded from somewhere within the old house. Lakin found himself hesitating, wavering in the following silence. It was a man's voice, he had thought, but now he wondered if it had been the muddled call of some bird. He put his hands into pockets and cleared his throat, walking slowly up the crumbling and cracked stairs and through the gaping front door.

Dust glimmered in a stream of light, reminding him of the finest sprinkle of snow. That intrusive sign of winter in the late fall. Of Lena and how much she had once loved the cold season: hot chocolate and tea, curling up together on the couch with nothing to keep them warm beneath the blankets except their yearning for each other. She would sit with a book and stare out at those sparse flakes, loving their presence as an indicator of winter's approach. Then she had started avoiding the windows, complaining of the numbness, and her books gathered dust.

"What are you doing here?"

The quiet voice came again, startling him out of his memory fog. He jumped, jerking away as he noticed a man standing only feet away from him. How had he not seen him before? Had he really been there, or had he entered from another room?

"I'm sorry," Lakin said, breathless with surprise. "I'm... I'm Lakin Douglas."

He offered a hand. The man was tall and thin, face slim and narrow with a pointed chin. His skin was sallow and eyes sunken, edged by sickly pink. There was something familiar about his blue eyes: somehow both kind and deceptive. His lips were a thin line, dry skin peeled up from the pale flesh.

"Simon Boyd," the man said, voice cracking. He did not take Lakin's offered hand.

"Wh... Mr. Boyd," Lakin said quickly, surprised. "I'm so sorry to have intruded on your property."

Simon didn't react to Lakin's apology, but instead said quietly, "Were you not sorry to trespass when you thought I was gone?"

Lakin was caught off guard but told himself he probably deserved that. This was private property, and there were signs posted on every boundary that signified that.

"I'm here to study the local wolves," Lakin explained. "I tracked them to the back of your property. I was just going to get some geographical notes for my report. I didn't plan on vandalizing or causing any disturbance. I am truly sorry for my trespassing."

Simon stared at him for several moments, lips moving as though he were saying something very hushed, and then he said, "Okay."

"Mr. Boyd, I have to say that I'm a fan of your own research..." Lakin started, feigning enthusiasm. The man's eyes moved up to him slowly, rising in jerky increments. He was strange, robotic. Something about his unnatural mannerisms unsettled Lakin further.

"My research?"

"I have read several of your articles online, from a few years ago. About the local mythology, the legends. I'd love to take you into town and buy you something to eat, or a cup of coffee, so we can talk about your theories."

"I can't go into that town."

Lakin faltered, but nodded. "Of course. Would you have time to talk to me now, then?"

"Here?"

"Yeah, if that's alright. I may never get the opportunity to meet you again."

"You won't."

"Okay. Great. Can you tell me about the legends surrounding the wolves here?"

Simon smiled, a very small gesture that looked painful, sympathetic. "Oh, the wolves. They're just a totem, you know? I never was really interested in the wolves, or any of that. The lycanthropes, you know, the werewolves. That was what I was interested in."

"I'm listening. Is the legend tied to the forest? The locust grove near the swamps at the back of your property?"

"You've been there?"

"No."

"Yes. This area is called Wolf Valley, you know, but not for the little animals you're looking for. There was a thing here. The native people that were here understood it; they valued it, they respected it. The thing needed a vessel, some kind of conduit or physical form. So the people would send in a woman, someone to mother that... thing."

Lakin had to lean in to hear Simon, and he asked, "Like a human sacrifice?"

"No... It didn't kill the host. In fact, it was said to grant them this spectacular power."

"The power to turn into a... werewolf?"

"Something like that... When the Europeans came to colonize this area, they wanted to take the thing from the indigenous people, but it had to be given. It had to be passed on, and only on this very specific ground."

"So like... holy ground or sacred soil or something?"

"No, there was nothing holy about it. The woman was as much gifted as cursed. She couldn't live with her family anymore; she had to become a creature of the woods. It was too dangerous to try to blend in. She would often protect her people from outsiders by using her power, or she would use it to exact revenge. But she would be tormented, hungry, passionate."

"A ticking time bomb," Lakin said. "So, let me guess, the European settlers somehow get the 'thing'."

Simon nodded. "Seduced the girl, convinced her to let him have the burden. He took it, wiped out the people. The entire population. What he didn't know, however, was that he couldn't leave the valley. He was trapped, and there was no one left to lure into the woods. His men abandoned him, and there he remained."

"So what happens if the host just... dies?"

"The thing waits. It is patient, as old things often are. People will come. They always have. The only way to make it leave the host is to kill the host or pass it on."

Lakin rocked back on his heels. "Mr. Boyd, from one rational man to another... do you really believe this?"

"You don't?"

Lakin shook his head. "I believe that there are explanations for everything. I love hearing an urban legend, a tall tale... but I don't believe them."

"Once, I didn't either. Then..."

Simon's eyes seemed to cloud, a curtain closing behind them somewhere and snuffing out any light. He was remembering something.

"What happened to your daughter out there, Mr. Boyd?"

He looked back to Lakin, face twisting into an expression of sorrow and terror. "It wanted her. The thing. So we did something terrible... we gave it someone else, but it still destroyed her mind and her body. She wasn't our little girl anymore."

"Who did you give to it?" Lakin asked curiously, wondering if he could trace it to a missing person. Had the Boyds, in their delirium, killed someone in the forest?

"You don't understand," Simon insisted, stepping so close to Lakin that he could smell his acrid breath. "I didn't believe either, but I do now. So you will."

Lakin took a step away from Simon, corkscrewing his lips into a forced smile. "Thanks for taking the time to talk to me, Mr. Boyd. I'm going to head out. I'm sorry again for trespassing. I'll be heading out."

"I can go with you... for the report you were here to do."

"No, I insist. It's fine. Thank you again... really. Truly."

"Don't you want to take a walk, Mr. Douglas?" Simon asked, even as Lakin briskly headed for the door.

"I'll take you there," Simon called again, voice barely rising in pitch. "I'll show you."

Lakin nearly stripped his gears trying to get out of the driveway, sweat beading on the back of his neck. He looked in his rearview as though he was afraid to see that vampiric-looking man standing just behind his car, but he could not see anything. He got his front left wheel jammed in a rut once, spinning for several minutes before he freed it. Any other time he would have used his winch, but he did not want to be out there. Not right now.

The vehicle lurched and spun gravel as it got back onto the highway, and he sped back towards the cabin.

Holly's truck was still parked out by the mailbox, the vehicle door standing open. As he passed by, he barely caught a glimpse of her in the field. She was running. He slammed on his breaks when he saw that she was being pursued by someone, and their pacing was far too fast to have been a game or leisure. He swung his door open so hard that it bounced back and hit his knee, turning to jerk his rifle out of the back as he jumped the barbed wire and headed across the field towards her.

The screams turned Lakin's blood icy and his feet leaden. He sprinted through the soft soil of the field as he saw Holly running towards her truck. She was making better distance than him, legs carrying her over all of the uneven ground like she knew its imperfections by heart. Something moved behind her in a dark blur and Lakin's mind couldn't, or wouldn't, identify it in that moment. He yelled her name, waving his arms to try to let her know he was there. What he had thought was a human pursuing her now looked much too large, much too...

His calves burned in protest as he continued across the pasture, stumbling down a small incline. His ankle screamed protests, head spinning as he nearly went head over heels. He slid down to rest at the bottom, grass stains on knees and backside seeping moisture through to his skin. Holly had fallen too, or been caught. Lakin's stomach sank as he looked up at her and over to the rifle that he'd dropped during his fall.

The animal was huge and unlike anything Lakin had ever seen before. His first thought was that it was some sort of bear. He'd seen plenty of animals that, due to emaciation, mange, or birth defects, looked like something horrific.

This was different.

The animal was at least nine feet tall on its rear legs, although it was currently crouched on all fours. Its face was undeniably canine, with a long snout and expressive features made for subtle communication. A short and tight, grey coat covered its face and burst into black-and-grizzle doublecoat along the rest of its body. Its limbs were long and powerful with rear paws that also looked canine. The front paws, however, like the one that rested on the sputtering body of Holly Gernt, were more like twisted primate hands. The phalanges were long and clawed with fully opposable thumbs. There was something eerie, human, too cunning about its eyes.

Lakin edged towards the rifle, where it lay just out of reach. The beast followed him with its eyes. It snarled at him, lowering its maw to inch towards Holly's face. She sobbed into the red clay, closing her eyes tightly as thick, elastic strands of saliva descended from its jaws. It seemed to be threatening him as he closed the space between himself and the gun, and it bore down on Holly's body even more forcefully. He thought he could hear her spine and ribs cracking under the weight. He told himself that the animal couldn't have any idea that the gun posed a threat. That it wasn't daring him to reach for it. If he didn't get that gun, Holly was dead.

He dove for the gun, and in one smooth movement the monster had wrenched Holly's head from her body, portions of tattered muscle and meat and spinal column hanging from the skull like the tendrils of a jellyfish. Lakin only had a moment to feel the repulsion and horror: a cold sweat and wave of nausea that had him suddenly gasping for breath through his lips. His hands were still steady as he turned and fell to a knee, using the other leg to stabilize the gun as he took a shot at the animal. The crack of gunfire echoed in the desolate field, the beast lurching up as the bullet hit its hide with a thud. Blood sprayed into the air, steaming in the morning chill.

Its jaws opened, dropping the human head as it barked, leaping towards Lakin but running past him. Lakin scrambled back onto his feet, looking over at Holly's decapitated body one last time before he took off after the animal.

It was gone.

Lakin followed the trail of blood until, all at once, it disappeared.

eighteen

Lakin sat inside Chitto's prewarmed Jeep. He knew that Chitto had left the heater on in an attempt to make it more comfortable inside, but Lakin was way too hot. The vents blew out musty air that smelled like both an old attic and burning plastic. He rolled his sleeves up, cranking the knob that should have adjusted the airflow, but found it was unresponsive. There must have been a certain quirk that made it work; secrets only known by its owner.

He watched through the fogged windshield as Chitto, tears running unchecked down his cheeks, stood talking to two police officers. He was grimacing, almost as though he was forcing the smile that showed all of his white teeth, but it wasn't a happy visage. He was struggling. Lakin was struggling, and he'd only met Holly once.

Chitto approached the Jeep, pausing outside of the door before he opened it and entered. He sat quietly for several seconds, taking deep and slow breaths. He wiped underneath both eyes and turned to look at Lakin. Lakin initially didn't look back over at him, staring instead down at his feet.

"What happened, Lakin?"

"It was an animal," he responded quietly.

"I know... I know that's what you told the police. I just... What kind of animal could do that? What kind of animal would do that?" Chitto's voice had risen in pitch, threatening to collapse into a sob entirely as a harsh breath escaped him. "I didn't want to see her. I wish I hadn't seen her."

"It was a bear... no... no, it was something else. Big as a bear, but a different animal. Stood up on its back legs, was at least eight or nine feet, standing erect."

"All we have out here are black bears, and they're usually not out this time of year... and I've never heard of one chasing someone down in a field and... she was decapitated, Lakin. Completely."

Lakin had a sudden, violent vision of the way her head had separated from her body. The way her face had tensed and reacted, eyes still blinking and lips still moving... the way that the beast had pulled her apart so effortlessly.

"I need to tell you something," Lakin said, forcing himself to make eye contact. "I need you to listen to me, and I need you to be honest with me."

Chitto looked at Lakin in a way he never had before. He looked suspicious, distrustful... maybe even a little scared.

Lakin's gut twisted and he ran a hand over his face. "You aren't going to believe me. I've got to get out of here."

Lakin pulled the handle on the door, but Chitto was suddenly lying across the seat, slamming the door shut.

"Try me," he said, voice sharp.

"Last night, Claire came to the cabin."

"For what?"

"That's just it. I don't know. She was being really weird... then Shaw came."

"He caught Claire with you at the cabin?"

"No... she disappeared. I don't know. I think she went out the back door. She said she walked."

"Walked? From where?"

"Listen, I don't know. Just let me finish. He found my glove, and I tried to come clean and tell him what happened but he just... he was threatening. He told me not to leave town until he was done investigating. Then when I woke up this morning, I thought I heard someone in the cabin. I went outside and found..."

He paused, looking away from him. Chitto in turn leaned towards him. "You found what, Lakin?"

"A little girl's shoe. Outside. There was blood on it."

"Shit. Okay, listen, Lakin. I like you, but now I want you to get out of my vehicle."

"Chitto, I don't have anything to do with any of this. I swear to God."

"What were you doing out here after finding that little girl's shoe? How are you showing up at Holly's, someone you just met, right as she gets her fucking head torn off by a bear?"

"I went to the Boyd place. I was just going to have a look around because it seems like no one wants me to go to that locust grove. When I got to the house, though, Simon Boyd was there. He was the creepiest person I have ever met. So I left in a hurry. I saw Holly as I went in, and when I came back out, she was running through the field, and I saw the animal after her. I got my gun and I was going to try to help her. I shot it... shot it with a thirty-aught. It barely flinched. I hit it."

"Please get out of my car," Chitto whispered, staring at his dark hands on the steering wheel as they gripped the fabric so tightly that it squeaked.

"You don't believe me," Lakin said in a flat voice that matched Chitto's low volume.

"I think you need help, Lakin. I think you need to talk to someone. I don't know if you have anything to do with any of this or if you even know what you're saying or doing. I know you've been going through a lot and you're under a lot of stress... but I need you to go now."

"Chitto, I have always been honest with you. Since we met, I've told you everything that's happened. I think someone is trying to frame me. I don't know who, or why... I think Shaw might be in on it."

"Again with the Shaw bullshit. He isn't even in town right now."

"Convenient."

"You know, you said you were always honest with me. But you aren't being honest with me now."

"About what?"

"Simon Boyd has been dead at least five years, Lakin. When he and his family moved off, he died in a car accident. Drunk driver, I heard. Either you're lying to me, or you think you saw a dead man... and he talked to you."

"I swear to God... There was a man there and he told me he was Simon Boyd. He told me some weird shit about werewolves and some spirit the indigenous people believed in. He told me about his daughter and everything. He was driving an old blue truck. Nice classic style, that real pale, powder blue. I could probably give you the freaking license place number if you'd just give me a second..."

Chitto interjected, "Blue truck?"

"Yeah."

He inspected Lakin carefully, eyes darting as he seemed to consider what he would say next. Lakin tried to be patient, feeling his heart pound in his chest. He needed someone on his side; he wanted Chitto to believe him.

"I'm going to say something, but I don't want you to take this as any kind of proof of anything. I just want us to be rational and level-headed."

Lakin nodded slowly. "Alright."

"The Lowells have a blue truck. Just like you described."

"This wasn't Shaw; this man said he was Simon Boyd... unless you think Shaw hired him to make me think I'm crazy."

"I just don't think he'd do something like that. Why would he? What would he have against you? What good would framing you for all this do? What would he possibly be hiding?"

"I don't know. I don't. I have never met him before I came here. I've never been to Rotten Fork before this."

"All I know is something is going on here. You say some big animal killed Holly, and you don't know what it was. I'm not saying I believe it was a... Jesus, I can't believe I'm even going to say this... I'm not saying I believe it was a werewolf, but there are things going on here that I can't explain; you can't explain. I think we need to be cautious, but I do not think it is Shaw behind all of this."

"Even now?"

Chitto shook his head. "Even now."

nineteen

Lakin pulled his SUV through the ice-slushed parking lot of the grocery store. He didn't feel right drinking water from the tap at the cabin anymore, imagining that the water that bubbled up from the ground might have been contaminated somehow by the bloated corpse of the groundskeeper or, maybe somewhere farther out in the forest where the spring was birthed, the body of little Dulcie Lloyd. When he slept last night, Lakin had worried about dreaming of Holly's severed head, the way her eyelids fluttered over her hazel irises even after it was totally severed from her body. The mangled mass of trachea and esophagus and gore and muscle and spinal column that hung like the strong roots of a plucked plant.

It was, for once, something he dreaded more than the dreams of Lena before her death. However, he instead dreamed that he found Dulcie's little body under the front steps of the porch, her shining pink shoes stained with blood. How unsurprised he would have been to find her that morning. He even leaned under the porch to check for her presence before he headed into town.

He hefted a case of bottled water into the shopping cart, followed by a sleeve of iced oatmeal cookies, more coffee, some beef jerky. The stress of yesterday led him to also grab a box of seltzer tablets for his stomach. There was no line at checkout, so he was in and out almost too quickly. The lady at the counter scanned his items slowly, looking up at him periodically with nervous eyes. When she did it enough times that he realized he wasn't just paranoid, he put on a soft smile.

"How are you today?" he asked politely, pushing the remainder of his items to the end of the belt for her.

"I'll need to scan your water," she said, voice quavering. She removed the scanning gun and walked around, keeping the buggy in between them as she scanned the pack and hurried back to her place.

"Is everything okay? You seem a little on edge." He looked around the store as though there might have been something else that was upsetting her.

"You're that guy from Obey, aren't you?"

Lakin tried to laugh. "Well, I am from the Obey Wildlife and Fisheries Laboratory. I don't know if I'm that guy from Obey."

Her face turned even more suspicious and she handed him his bags. "It'll be twenty-four sixty-two."

He handed her two worn twenties from his wallet and she spoke again, "Everybody thinks you're a serial killer."

Lakin was surprised, dropping the coins she handed him onto the floor, making the smallest noise as they struck the tile. The woman seemed annoyed by the sound, looking around as though she was afraid someone might have heard it. There were just a handful of other shoppers in the building, and none of them looked up.

"I shouldn't have said that," she said, clearing her throat.

"Why?" Lakin asked, and immediately the woman began shaking her head from side to side. She held up a hand to stop his question but he continued, "If you're going to say something like that to me, I want to know why. I will stand here... all day."

She chewed the inside of her lip with her front teeth and then sniffled her nose, little dry inhalations. "You came into town and people started dying... real mysterious deaths. And right after... I mean, we all heard your wife died too. You know how this looks. If you aren't a... you know, if you aren't, you still have to know how this looks."

Lakin didn't respond, staring at the woman for several long seconds before he gathered his bags and pushed the buggy out the front door. He didn't know why he cared what these people thought of him in this town. When he had figured out everything here, he would leave and never look in the direction of Rotten Fork again.

He stopped in his tracks in the middle of the parking lot, noticing that parked alongside his vehicle was the blue truck. It was still running, exhaust creating a cloud behind it as it grumbled there. He could see a figure inside the cab, and they seemed to notice him as well. Initially, Lakin couldn't make himself move, frozen to the spot. It wasn't until a car approached behind, honking briefly, that he jumped back to awareness and continued to his own vehicle.

The truck shut off and the door creaked loudly as it opened. Across the top of the cab, he saw Claire's face peek over at him. She was beaming, a wide grin that showed all of her teeth. It was a grand contrast to the woman who had come into his cabin uninvited. He wondered at this moment whether she'd ever been there at all. Had it been some malevolent spirit? Some sort of doppelganger? His own mind creating a chance encounter?

"Hey, neighbor," Claire said, jumping down from the truck and coming around to meet him at the side of his car.

"Good afternoon, Mrs. Lowell. That's a really nice truck Shaw's got there. Did he restore that on his own?"

She looked back over her shoulder, laughing. "No, no. She's all mine. I bought her in this condition, though. I'm not handy like that."

Lakin looked over the truck again. "Is Shaw around? I've been needing to talk to him about a few things."

"No, he's out of town... has been for several days. Has some business he's got to deal."

"Did you hear about Holly?"

"Of course I have. It's a small town... everyone knows everything, Mr. Douglas."

Lakin noted how there was not a single sign of remorse or sorrow on Claire's face. He reminded himself, however, that Shaw had cheated on her with Holly, or so the rumors told. He got the impression that, despite her bubbly demeanor, Claire was probably pretty cutthroat. He imagined that she wasn't going to mourn the death of one of her husband's mistresses.

Then again, he also remembered that Marie told him Claire was 'no angel' either. Some relationships just functioned that way, he supposed. A healthy dose of promiscuity.

"What do you need to talk to Shaw about?" she asked, voice curious.

"Oh, just some... stuff," Lakin said, shoving his groceries into the passenger seat and scooting the buggy into the single return available.

"Any stuff I could help with?"

"Oh, no... I don't think so."

"I could come by later," she suggested, waving her hand in the air.

"That's alright. I have some things I need to get done. I'm having a late lunch with Chitto, too."

"Well, if you change your mind..." she said, walking away. She turned around for a few steps, waving at him. "Bye."

Lakin waved awkwardly at her and got into his vehicle. It wasn't a lie that he was going to lunch with Chitto. He hadn't seemed comfortable coming to the cabin, and honestly Lakin didn't blame him. He instead offered to meet him at the general store for a sandwich. Chitto had called early that morning and told Lakin he had something interesting to show him. Something that could give them clues to what happened.

When he arrived at the general store, he stopped at the counter to place his order: a vanilla jar shake, a BLT with mayo, and fries. He found Chitto by the wall and seated himself across from him.

"What's this color called?" Lakin said, motioning to Chitto's hot-pink fingernails.

Chitto didn't seem as friendly as usual. "I don't know. Pretty-in-Paris Pink or something."

"What's up?" Lakin dropped his tone to convey he was ready to be serious.

"So I went back to Holly's last night," Chitto said quietly, not even looking up at the waitress as she delivered Lakin's milkshake, in a fudge-rimmed mason jar, and his sandwich. He suddenly felt self-conscious when he realized that Chitto hadn't ordered anything at all.

"Why?"

"I just wanted to make sure I didn't see anything suspicious inside and... I don't know. You've got in my head, I guess. I just wanted to look at her security cameras and see if I saw any sign of Shaw. I still do not believe he's involved. I'm not saying that. I'm just wanting to check into everything. Holly was an experienced outdoorswoman. She has ridden horses on overnight trips in some of the roughest areas. She has been face-to-face with the worst of people and animals and she has always come out on top. I just can't imagine her..."

He stopped, putting his hand to his mouth.

"It's alright," Lakin said, reaching over to squeeze Chitto's other arm.

"So I looked at the cameras. I watched hours and hours of it. The barn, the corral, the back of the house. The only weird thing I saw was this..."

He pulled out his cell phone, loading a video that was a recording of another screen. Lakin could tell that the video was pixelated even before it had to be translated through a second screen. It was very difficult to make out what was going on.

The clip was blue and black, probably taken at night. For several seconds, Lakin didn't see anything, but then a figure entered the frame from the top.

It was a woman, and she was nude. She walked slowly through the path of the camera, stopping long enough to lean in one direction as though she had heard something, and then she changed her path towards whatever had gotten her attention.

"What is Holly doing outside, naked?" Lakin asked.

"I don't know," Chitto said, shaking his head. "She never did drugs or anything like that. She could put away the alcohol, but I just can't imagine her drunk, wandering around the ranch, naked."

"What's on her shoulder there?" Lakin asked, pointing at Holly's shoulder.

"I saw that too. I was wondering if she was hurt."

"When was this?"

"The night before she died."

"Do you know... do you remember if she was hurt when they took her body?"

"There was so much blood. I don't know."

"Do you think... do you think it could've been like some kind of bite or something?"

"Like what? Like this werewolf you're after?" Chitto scoffed. "If this thing is real, I don't think you survive a bite."

"I'm just saying... there's clearly something there. And how she's walking... maybe she was hurt. She isn't walking like Holly usually did, is she?"

"I guess not," Chitto agreed. "I'll see if I can get in touch with the medical examiner. If they can pin it on an animal, you know that's their motive. So he'd be happy to tell me it was a bite."

"Do that. Get any info you can."

Chitto nodded, reaching over to grab a fry from Lakin's plate. He dipped it in the whipped cream atop the shake and then ate it.

"Will you go with me back to the Boyd place? I just want someone to stay behind with the truck, that way no one can sneak up on me. We can go tomorrow morning."

"Are you going into the grove?"

"That's the plan... just in and out. That's all."

Chitto inhaled, eyes moving from Lakin's face down to his plate of fries as he let the breath out in a sigh. "Alright. In and out."

twenty

Chitto and Lakin didn't talk much on the way to the Boyd place. Even empty, the house was eerie and foreboding. Lakin was satisfied to still see the tracks of the truck that had been there, some proof that he hadn't imagined the encounter with the supposedly dead Simon Boyd after all. He put the vehicle in park, leaving the engine on.

"How far is the walk, you think?"

Chitto motioned beyond the house. "It's straight back; you'll go into the tree line and keep going. There's a trail but it may be grown up by now. The perimeter is marked by orange flags and private property signs. I'd say fifteen minutes if you're walking on."

"I'll walk on then," Lakin agreed, unbuckling and retrieving his rifle out of the back.

"Be careful out there."

"If I take too long or if someone shows..."

"Oh, I'll walk home." Chitto laughed. "I don't need your permission. I will not step foot in there to look for you."

"You superstitious too?"

"Just because I don't believe in something doesn't mean I want to poke it with a stick."

Lakin laughed as he got out and walked around the back of the truck, where he had a tarp strapped down over some equipment: camping items, a bagged tripod, and some other things that didn't fit in the cab. He retrieved a snake hook and headed out, using the hook like a walking stick as he crossed the unmaintained back lawn of the homestead.

He remembered seeing it from a distance before and was even more amazed at how expansive the backyard of this home had once been. There were remnants of a fountain and stone path, benches, a meager rock wall. A man-made pond had taken on a life and ecosystem of its own, although Lakin thought he still saw the orange scales of koi or goldfish shimmer low beneath the surface as he walked by.

The walk to the forest itself was not far, and the dark trees welcomed him inside. He tried to remain on a straight line of travel, keeping an eye out for the old trail. After tripping over logs and sloshing through the increasingly damp ground, he finally stumbled upon the trail... except, it was not in a state of disrepair as Chitto had warned.

On the contrary, the dirt path was mostly clear, only covered by a few late-falling leaves or twigs from the trees above. It was lined with sizable rocks, and he was able to follow it ahead with his eyes. It wound around through the woods and up a hill before disappearing on the other side.

Lakin mounted the incline, and when he came up on the vantage point, he noticed that it went into a swampy valley where the tree trunks possessed thorns that were three or four inches long and thicker than his fingers. He recognized them as honey locusts. This was the place.

He took note of the tattered, faded orange tags wrapped around the trunks of several smaller trees, and then the barely readable NO TRESPASSING signs scattered among them.

Lakin descended the hill, entering the swampy ground. There was an immediate odor of natural decay, and he took note that the air was much denser. He thought that these things could be partly responsible for the phenomenon of hallucinations and other neurological issues that people were experiencing when they came here. The sensation that you were somewhere else; something else.

In the damp soil, Lakin saw the paw prints of the small wolves and other forest animals. His hand clutched the strap of the rifle on his shoulder for some semblance of security, and he pressed farther into the grove. Between his fingers he sampled one of the thorns on a nearby locust, finding that it was not brittle yet. In some areas it was difficult to avoid bumping his arms on them as he continued down the narrowing path.

Ahead, the path widened into a circular area where Lakin noted a stack of stones. It was not uncommon to see these out in the wild, especially near rivers and streams. Young people didn't understand how detrimental these could be to native fish and amphibians, who could become crushed beneath them or otherwise disturbed by the movement of their environment.

There was something unusual about this arrangement, however. It was covered in moss as though it had been here for some time, and atop the stack of stones was a necklace. Lakin approached warily, reaching forward to touch the lichen-covered necklace. He thought that the beads might have been made out of bone. Whatever it was, he was sure it was very old.

The smell of natural gasses from the swamp was strong, and a variety of mushrooms and slime molds grew on nearly every surface.

Beneath him the soggy earth was swallowing his boots. He started walking back to more solid ground, abandoning the stone altar. As he approached the trail, he noticed something move among the trees up the hill. Lakin froze, nearly falling forward into the swamp. He blinked once, twice. Had he really seen it? It was something that he initially would have dismissed as just another tree, another part of the repeating pattern of forest materials. He was sharp in the wild like this; always keen on his surroundings. You had to be. How had he not heard the thing, or the person, approach?

More hesitant now, Lakin started moving up the hill to where the thing had stood, and he found indentions in the soil. Long feet, like a person's... but barefoot, and not enough detail to tell much. He looked around, eyes scanning the area. From here, he could see for several yards in any direction, but he didn't find anything there.

In the distance, he heard the sound of something howling... an unearthly moan that echoed around him before finishing in a gravelly shriek. The closest animal that Lakin could attribute it to was perhaps a European red stag, which wasn't realistic. Maybe it was an elk bugling himself into hoarseness.

Lakin felt lightheaded; the air was just too heavy, and the smell of the swamp was overpowering. Rotten, he thought. Like the fork of the river that the area was named for. He took deep inhales through his nose and out through his mouth as he started following the stone-lined trail, but soon he was stumbling.

"Come on," he told himself, voice tight in his throat. "Not too far now."

The trees were moving around him, and he thought he could see a dark figure on the trail ahead of him, moving with the breeze as it approached. He was suffocating; his throat and nostrils burned, and his chest heaved without filling his lungs with air. He raised a hand to the figure, as though he might be able to motion to them for help.

Lakin was on his knees, then his hands and knees, then on his stomach, and then everything was black.

When Lakin regained consciousness, he found himself still on the trail in the forest. His entire body ached; his head throbbed. He struggled onto his feet and squinted into the darkening sky. He had been out for hours.

"Shit," Lakin breathed, hurrying along the trail. He didn't slow down until he was crossing the boundaries of the Boyd place, circling around the old home where his truck still sat, idling in the dark. He wasn't surprised to find the truck empty, because there would have been no way that Chitto would have stayed this long, but he would have expected him to shut the truck off.

The gas hand was leaning on E, and Lakin struggled into the front seat, throwing his hook and rifle into the passenger seat as he peeled out of the driveway and onto the highway. He really needed to get some gas, but he was so tired and so thirsty. He needed to take something for his headache.

As he drove, he dialed Chitto's number, but it went to voicemail. He said: "Man, I'm sorry. I know you're probably pissed. I don't know what happened... I passed out on the trail. I think the theory about there being some noxious gasses in the swamps could be true. It's likely causing people to have hallucinations, and they're losing consciousness. Who knows. I think I could go back and get some water samples and take them back to the lab. I don't know much about water but... You know, we'll just talk about this tomorrow. Give me a call or text later, alright?"

He hung up the phone, and continued the drive back to the cabin. He pulled the truck in front of the driveway, parking it parallel to the road by the walkway. As he descended the steps he paused, getting an eerie sensation that he was being watched or that he wasn't alone. He rubbed his hand on the back of his neck, feeling the cold sweat there. He jogged back to the truck, pulling his rifle out and taking it with him. Then he hurried inside and locked the door behind him... deadbolt, too.

He moved to pour a bottle of water into a glass and then dropped in a seltzer tablet. It fizzed as it sank to the bottom, bubbles rising to the surface and creating a static hiss that sounded like rain.

v.

She used to set her houseplants out on rainy days, loving the way they smelled when she brought them in after a storm. He had started associating the sound of the rain on the roof with a damp heaviness in the air and the scent of their potting soil when it was watered by the heavens.

The plants were her canary in the mineshaft: when she started to fade, they died first. It was a clue, a desperate plea for help, one that Lakin neglected to notice.

He didn't realize.

He just bought her more plants.

twenty-one

Lakin woke up the next morning, later than usual. He knew by the way that the sun was shining through the cabin's windows and by how comfortably warm it was inside, even without the fire. He reached over to unplug his cell phone, turning the screen on to view the time: 12:30.

He hadn't slept that late since college.

There were two missed calls, both from Shaw, and a message from him that read, *Call me, we need to talk*. He wondered why Shaw hadn't come straight to the cabin and banged on the door until he answered, but he supposed that just meant it wasn't anything serious.

He also noticed that Chitto had read his message but hadn't responded. He was probably pissed. Lakin dialed his number, but after several rings it went to his voicemail again. He hung up without leaving one, instead sending another text that simply read: *Are you up?*

The rifle propped beside the foot of the bed was a reminder of the scare he had yesterday. He was surprised by how far away the incident felt already. Maybe he should go into town and have a checkup, especially after what had happened.

Lakin dialed Tyler and was thankful to hear his chipper voice on the other end of the phone after a single ring. "Hey, Lakin. How's it going up there?"

"Not good... How is the proposal coming along?" Lakin said, rushing into the question.

"It's pending approval now. I think I will just head on up there next weekend to keep you company. I think at this point it's just getting someone to sign the check. What's going on? You said it isn't good?"

"Too much to tell you over the phone. I went into this... I don't know, locally sacred swamp. Honey locusts growing like crazy. I think there are some weird things going on there... I think it could be contributing to some of the local legends of disappearances, mania, werewolves. The whole nine."

"Are you thinking like methane poisoning or something?"

"Exactly, or something fungal, maybe. I'm not sure. Will you see if Wilhelmina would be willing to check out some water and soil samples if I can get out there to collect some?"

"Yeah, if you're that determined to crush this town's local legends." He laughed.

"It's more than that. There's just... there's a lot going on."

He saw movement outside of the window and noticed the scraggly orange cat moving around behind his truck. It coiled itself up, tail wrapping around its body as it sat on the ground just behind his truck bed. A 'loaf'— Lena used to call it that when the cats would curl their tiny feet up under the body and relax. He noticed it had settled down like this to lap something up off the ground underneath his truck.

"Hey, I gotta go," Lakin said. "There's this feral cat, and I think the truck is leaking antifreeze."

"Alright, talk soon," Tyler said.

Lakin tossed the phone onto the bed and hurried outside. He knew antifreeze was toxic to dogs; did it have the same ill effects on cats? He hissed at the cat between his front teeth as he approached, trying to shoo it away from the toxic puddle.

It trilled, moving up to rub on his legs once before returning to the puddle to drink. He reached down to retrieve the cat and gently placed it in the opposite direction. The cat grumbled low in its throat at him but started walking away from the cabin and into the woods.

Lakin noticed now that it was not a pooling of antifreeze or oil but instead something dark and viscous. As he stared, he saw another thick drop fall to the center, not rippling but instead making an audible pat before it merged into the growing puddle. He looked up at the lowered truck bed, and from beneath the tarps there he saw a hand, fingers extending down like they were reaching, coagulating blood dripping slowly from the fingertips.

His horror glued him to the spot, legs made of lead, gut icy. It wasn't until he gathered the courage to reach up and move the tarp that he noticed the dark fingers had bright pink, chipped nail polish.

twenty-two

Lakin was rocking in the stiff chair, foot tapping audibly against the floor under the table. He was having trouble pinpointing the emotions that were rising up in his chest. He was sick, he was angry. He had been through many situations in life where he could have lashed out or had this overflow of negative emotion, but he'd always found himself somehow incapable of reaching that level.

Now it was overwhelming.

The door across from him opened slowly and Shaw entered. He looked tired: dark circles under his eyes, beard scraggly and untrimmed. His hair was mussed, and Lakin wondered whether underneath his leather aviator jacket were nothing but layman's clothes. He smelled like beer and aftershave, the smell reaching Lakin even at a distance. In his hands were two cups of coffee, only half filled. He set them on the table, sliding one across to Lakin.

"Why am I here, Shaw?" Lakin asked, sitting up against the desk. The edge of it ground against his ribs. "You know I didn't do anything. You know I wouldn't hurt Chitto."

Shaw sat down; casual, calm, cool, and collected. If he was stressed out in any way, he wasn't showing it. He pulled a pen out of his pocket and laid a pad of paper on the tabletop.

"Listen, I don't think you did it," Shaw said, cordial. "Why would you?"

"Then why are you questioning me?"

Shaw shrugged his shoulders. "Procedure. That's all. Nothing personal. You're new in town. Ever since you've been here, people showing up dead... three of them found by you personally. One fresh in your truck after you claim you had an episode of... what? Amnesia? A black out? If I didn't at least bring you in for questioning, people would tear you apart. Small-town justice, you know. Especially over Chitto; everyone loved Chitto."

"Everyone except you."

Shaw raised his brows, laying his pen down as he leaned forward across the table. Lakin, who was rarely confrontational, swallowed back his nerves and mimicked the action, meeting Shaw's gaze in the center of the table. He didn't know what had gotten into him; he would have never had the guts to do this. Maybe it was the compounding of everything that had happened, but he was going to ride out this bravery as far as it would take him.

"I never said I didn't like Chitto. I introduced you to Chitto. We go way back. We... went way back."

"I don't see a lot of mourning here. I'm no cop and I don't claim to be, but it seems to me like you have a little history with everyone who's wound up dead. How's that for a motive?"

Shaw laughed, but he also broke eye contact. He looked at his folded hands on the table, pursing his lips together before turning his attention back to Lakin. "This is a county of fewer than eight hundred people, Lakin, and not even a quarter of those people live in Rotten Fork. Everybody's got history with everybody."

"Alright then, what was the history with Chitto? Why weren't you friends with him like everyone else? Don't think I didn't notice how everyone loved him, sought him out... but not you. I think he was intimidated by you. Why? Why was that?"

Shaw's voice dropped in volume. "Sometimes somebody knows too many of your dirty little secrets for you to be best buddies. You got any of those, Douglas? Any skeletons hanging around in your closet? I know there are. I can see them in your eyes."

Lakin nodded, a soft smile slowly moving across his lips. "Of course. The difference is, someone knew all of your dark spots, didn't they? I have plenty, just like everyone else. Some of the shit I carry is so heavy, you can't even imagine. Where were you when Holly was murdered? Convenient that you weren't around."

"Trust me, you want to be a little more polite with me. I'm the only person on your side right now."

"You're on my side? You?" Lakin found himself laughing, voice hysterical.

"The only friend you have in the whole damn world as far as you're concerned."

"Unless you're going to arrest me, I want out of here."

"Bette at the general store says the day that Chitto was suspected to have been murdered, he was having lunch with you. She said he was acting really nervous, not like himself. Said he didn't even order any food, didn't tip the waitress, didn't talk to anyone. She said he didn't even buy his regular snuff."

"We were both on edge. He knew something was—"

"You're the last person to see him alive. Then he's dead in the back of your truck."

"Why would I report a crime I committed?"

"Like I said before... I don't think you did it. I don't think you're capable of it."

Lakin sat back, chair legs fussing across the floor with a little chuffing squeak. He wanted to tell him that he didn't know what he was capable of. That he underestimated him. He barely caught himself in time to stop the words from tumbling out. He had to get out of here. He was spiraling out of control.

"What else do you want from me, Shaw?" Lakin asked.

"I'm going to need you to stay in town until we get this figured out, but I also don't want you in town. It's making people nervous, and frankly I worry about your safety. Just hang out at the cabin, where I know I can find you, until we get the investigation of Chitto's death sorted out."

"My safety?" Lakin scoffed.

Shaw sat back in his chair. "People already know where you're staying. That's dangerous enough. You don't want someone sneaking in there, poisoning your coffee, do you?"

Lakin didn't respond but instead settled back into his chair. Shaw nodded. "Okay, good. We have an understanding. Stick around, we'll get this figured out in a jiffy. I'll get one of the guys to take you back home, I'm afraid you're going to be without a vehicle for a bit."

"You can't take my truck!" Lakin insisted, rising to stand.

"I can..." Shaw said, voice calm as he strode to the door. "And I will. It's evidence. There's a story there, and we've got to read it first."

"I don't need a ride, I can walk."

Shaw laughed, "You're serious? Do you know how far it is to the cabin from here?"

"I do. Don't underestimate me, Mr. Lowell."

"I think that's all I have been doing," Shaw admitted, and left the room.

As the emptiness of the room swelled in Shaw's absence, Lakin allowed himself to start shaking nervously.

twenty-three

Lakin thought that Shaw did underestimate how far he was capable and willing to walk. He wasn't going back to the cabin yet. He had spent a majority of the day at the station waiting: hours and hours that felt like seconds compared to the half hour or less he'd spent face-to-face with Shaw. So as he started walking out of town, the sun was already starting to go down. It retired early this time of year.

He could have just kept walking until he was outside of the county, hoping that someone would pick him up or that he would stumble upon some kind of establishment where he could warm up and hang out until he found a ride. Instead, however, Lakin was walking down Holly Gernt's driveway. He was going to try to get a better look at the security footage, maybe even snap a picture of the screen on his phone. He wondered if Tyler could clear up the image for him, and maybe it would offer a better view of the bite on Holly's shoulder. What was he going to do even if he did confirm it was some sort of large canid bite wound? Holly was dead, and this wouldn't bring her back.

But it would help Lakin; it would confirm that he wasn't crazy, that he'd really seen that massive creature tear Holly's head off. It was something she'd encountered before, maybe something she thought she could tame or reason with somehow.

Lakin stepped up on the side porch of Holly's house. The bulb that would have once glowed a hazy yellow-orange to allow better visibility was cold and dark. The door wasn't locked, but there was one strip of caution tape half-heartedly stuck midway across the door facing and a note that stated it was private property, and no entrance was permitted.

It was funny how a place could feel alive, sentient.

As Lakin opened the door to Holly's house, he thought he could hear the house pop and groan. A great inhale that was rasping, dying without the heart: the humans who had called it home. The air inside was cold but still contained a sort of static and electricity from motion. He could feel it cause his hair to stand on end as his boots shuffled across the low-pile carpet.

He wasn't worried about being caught there, since no one else really had any reason to show up at the dead woman's house. Her family had been in, taken everything they wanted, for the most part. He was pleased to see that the surveillance system remained on the desk by the couch, and photos of Holly and her horses still adorned the walls.

Lakin noted that the system was fairly aged, and not just by the yellowing plastic case of the various green-tinted screens, but by the fact that there was a physical disk drive. He had been expecting an SD card slot, but instead he was presented with a CD-ROM.

He reached for the eject button, and then a stream of light spilled across the living room from outside.

Lakin flinched and stumbled backwards, tripping over the edge of the rigid couch as he was momentarily blinded by the headlights. He got back onto his feet, crouching in order to avoid casting a shadow that the driver might see.

He considered rushing down the hallway to try to find a back door somewhere but instead resorted to shoving himself into a closet full of coats and jackets. It smelled like the barn and the horses, leather and sweat.

He realized too late that the closet didn't have a proper door but rather a set of rustic louver doors.

Shaw shoved the front door open, bringing in a cool breath of night that chilled Lakin where he hid. He was afraid to move. Every inhale he took, no matter how slight, caused the hangers that held coats and jackets to squeak across the metal pole. He backed up slowly, trying to pin himself into a corner as Shaw looked around like he heard something; knew someone else was there. Lakin was familiar with that feeling, the sensation that you weren't alone. It was interesting how the presence of another human could be detected by some primal sense.

Abandoning any obvious suspicion, Shaw began pressing buttons on the surveillance system and Lakin's heart sank. Shaw was going to get the disk before he did. After pressing eject several times, however, he and Shaw both realized that the disk was gone. Someone had taken it.

"Fuck!" Shaw yelled and then screamed loudly to the ceiling. Lakin flinched, having to clamp his eyes shut to keep from making any sort of startled noise.

Shaw pressed some buttons. Lakin could barely see what he was doing through the slatted closet door. He was trying to review footage, maybe. Shaw's phone rang, the shrill bell tones singing through the quiet house. He pulled it out of his pocket and put it to his ear, regaining immediate composure. "Hey, honey. Yeah, I'm just working. I'm not... I'm not with anyone. I'm working by myself. For Christ's sake, Claire, yes I'm sure there's someone in the fucking building other than me, but I'm not with anyone. No, I know exactly what you meant."

Shaw exited the house, slamming the door behind him. Lakin didn't move until he heard Shaw's tires spinning as he pulled down the driveway.

"Trouble in paradise..." Lakin whispered, finding some comfort in the quiet of his own voice.

Lakin knew there was only one reasonable explanation for the missing disk. Chitto had taken it, knowing that someone would come here looking for it to try and destroy the evidence that might have been there. He had some satisfaction in knowing that it was Shaw who had shown up. Chitto's house was only a short distance up the road. If no one was there, he could try to find it before Shaw did.

The walk through the dark field to Chitto's house was unnerving. Lakin had the same sinking feeling Shaw had felt in the house: that someone was there, watching him. Someone who was hidden away but still very present. He more than once turned to look into the dark and even the twinkling night sky, a waning moon providing a small amount of cool light.

Just before he crossed onto Chitto's property, he passed over a little side road that cut to what appeared to be a popular dumping spot. The moon illuminated dozens of shattered tube televisions, tattered furniture, and piles of glistening colored bottles with an eerie glow. He hurried into the overgrown grass that peeked through what little snow was left in the shadowy areas of Chitto's lawn.

He noticed the fluffy dog lying dead in the yard at the end of its chain. There was an overturned bowl of food and a frozen bowl of water. He wondered if no one had been there to check on the dog or if someone had killed it. A little paranoid, he thought, to worry that Chitto's killer had come for the dog too.

He was not as lucky with the front door as he had been at Holly's house. He resorted to breaking a window to get inside, as he could not kick down the trailer's front door. The crunch of glass beneath him only amplified his guilt. Even knowing that Chitto was gone, he still felt wrong breaking into his home.

The interior of the home smelled like sage and sweetgrass, and the air was still warm. A space heater sat in the middle of the living room on a colorful braided rug, just barely covering a worn section of carpet. The metal surface of the heater still popped and clicked as it cooled, suggesting that it had only recently run out of fuel.

Lakin moved to the speckled countertop, sifting through the scattered papers. He didn't have to look for very long, thankfully, before he found two items of interest: a cell phone with a large letter 'H' in cow print on the cover, and a compact disk. The CD was in a piece of folded and taped paper and was unlabeled, but Lakin had no doubt that it was the footage from Holly's security system.

He tucked the CD into the pocket of his jacket and then lifted the phone. With the upward motion, the screen came on, a red battery emblem in the corner flashing threateningly as the screen dimmed. Lakin had to make a quick decision on whether or not he wanted to look at the contents of the phone. The thought that Chitto had definitely looked through the contents before he died encouraged Lakin to swipe up.

The background was of a spindly legged, buckskin foal, and there were a few game apps and the general social media widgets. He clicked the text messages first, scrolling through the recent messages that ranged from spam to innocent communications. He clicked on LOWELL when it showed up, finding a consistent string of messages between Holly and Shaw. Some of them were platonic enough: 'hey, what's up,' 'have you heard anything about so-and-so,' 'can I borrow a horse to look for a lost hiker.' Then some of the late-night messages were suggestive; Holly had sent a picture of herself naked in front of a long mirror. Those were recent. Nothing came across that suggested Shaw had been there when she'd died or met up with her in person any time lately.

The phone blinked off, bathing Lakin and the room around him in darkness. He laid it back on the counter with the monogram facing up.

twenty-four

Lakin could have gone to bed as soon as he got back to the cabin. He was exhausted, both from the lengthy trek from Holly's and from the close call with Shaw. He didn't have time for that, though; he needed to keep moving forward with unraveling the mystery of this town and whatever was going on in it. There was, undeniably, something natural occurring that he couldn't explain. Whatever had killed Holly was a real, in-the-flesh animal. A creature that could be found; a creature that could be killed, if needed. He also knew, however, that if there was one, there was likely an entire species out there. How? Something that size would devastate a local ecosystem. Unless...

Unless it really was a werewolf. He knew that logically this wasn't even a possibility, but there was still so much that could not be explained. But if Shaw was the wolf, why hadn't he killed Lakin yet? He'd had plenty of opportunity, plenty of motive. Why did all of this just start now?

Lakin had an even more sinister thought, one that he tried to shove away any time it bubbled to the surface. The thought that, maybe, it really was him. Everything started when he'd come into town. Had he lost his mind when he'd lost Lena? He still remembered his friend and paramedic, Haribo, sitting with him on the frozen ground, arm wrapped around his shoulders.

"I'm going to deal with this, Lakin. Okay?" That's what he'd said to him, and while Lakin babbled and sobbed with frosted saliva and tears on his face, Haribo had done just that. Haribo had taken care of everything. He had covered Lena's body, that giant gory eye that had formed through her skull disappearing beneath the zipper of a black bag. He reminded Lakin that Lena was sick and that he had done everything he could to help her. That he couldn't blame himself for what had happened in the end. Haribo then helped them push her covered body into the ambulance. The red and blue lights illuminating the dawn, but no siren to signify an urgency of transport. He had hated that the day had gone on. That this had happened so early, and that everything just went on without her. As the ambulance had driven away, leaving him truly alone, Lakin felt something. That dark heaviness that had consumed her. The shadow of doubt and death.

He shook away the thoughts and sat down at his laptop, inserting the cold CD into the drive.

He worked quickly to trim a small section of the clip in which Holly was visible. She was confused — maybe even scared — as she stood naked in the snow outside of her home. He paused the clip on her face, wondering what it was that had driven her to do something so bizarre. She had looked and behaved normally, as best he could tell, when he'd passed her on his way to the Boyd place. She'd smiled, waved, and continued about her work. Nothing like this.

He attached the clip to an email to Tyler and then dialed him up on the phone. Tyler answered the phone after a single ring, voice eager, "Lakin? I tried to call you, had me a little worried."

"I need you to be sitting down for this," Lakin said quietly.

"Okay... sitting."

"When I got off the phone with you, I went outside and found Chitto's body in the back of my truck."

There was a long silence. It lingered for such an amount of time that Lakin took the phone away from his ear to make sure the call hadn't disconnected. He let Tyler continue to process it, until he finally spoke again.

"The guy that's been nice to you? He's... Jesus Christ, he's dead?"

"Yeah, and he was in my truck," Lakin repeated. "I was the last person to see him alive. He was with me in the woods, when I blacked out. He was sitting in the truck waiting on me. When I got back there, he was gone. I thought he'd bailed and went home, but someone killed him and put him in the back of my truck."

"Lakin, you've got to get out of there. This isn't a little small-town drama anymore. This is getting dangerous."

"The sheriff told me that until I am cleared as a suspect for Chitto's murder, I can't leave town."

"That's just... okay. Okay. You know what? I'm going to come up there. I'll talk to Jada and I'll take a couple of days off."

"Tyler, no. I'm just going to lie low, I'm not going to go anywhere or talk to anyone."

"I'll be there in a day or two. I won't take 'no' for an answer. You need someone to watch your back, someone who knows you aren't capable of killing someone."

"I did do something kind of stupid... I broke into that dead woman's house."

"What dead woman? Lakin, what's going on?"

Lakin took a deep breath and exhaled. He realized now that he hadn't told Tyler about Holly. He hadn't told him about the animal.

"I can't believe I forgot to tell you."

How could he have forgotten that? If nothing else, witnessing a death was noteworthy. Witnessing a death caused by an unidentifiable animal was definitely something one mentioned in their line of work. That would be what most interested Tyler.

"I'm sorry," Lakin started again. "My head isn't right lately. This place really has me messed up. When you get up here, I'm going to get you up to speed. Right now, though, I sent a little video clip to your email."

He heard what sounded like a desk chair squeaking, then rolling across the floor. "Okay, yeah. I see it."

"There's a woman in this video, and it looks like she's hurt. Can you do a still and clear up the image for me?"

"I can try. Depending on the file type, this probably isn't ever going to be crisp and detailed, but I'll do what I can... Why is she naked? I really don't like this, Lakin."

"Maybe a psychotic break or something. I really don't know. The woman in the video is dead."

"Christ..."

"I'll catch you up when you get here. I promise."

"Alright. Well, keep in touch until I get there. I'll see when I can get off to come up there. Keep your door locked... Do I sound like your mother yet?"

"Yeah, I've been keeping it locked, but I still get this weird feeling that someone is coming in while I'm gone. Little things. Vibes."

"Don't drink from open containers," Tyler laughed.

"Will do. Talk to you soon."

He laid his phone to the side, shutting the laptop. He locked the front door and peered carefully out of the window for any signs of life. He didn't see anyone, anything. He climbed into bed, burying himself beneath the sheets until it was wholly dark. He went to sleep quickly, under that magic spell that the cabin seemed to have: a deep, somnolent powder of preternatural properties.

He thought that he woke once, the inky black of the cabin's interior purged by a muted red-and-purple glow. A jellyfish was suspended in the air, its tendrils leaving wet trails along the floor as it floated across the width of the room. Not until its gentle spiral turned it to face him did he see that it was Holly's head. The tendrils pulsed, pushing out more and more volumes of coagulated blood and chunks of flesh to the floor, until her mouth opened and she screamed.

Lakin woke for real after that, eyes popping open to the comforting and empty night. He noticed that the refrigerator door was slightly ajar, the fan inside working overtime to keep everything cool and emanating its pale yellow light. He trudged slowly across the cold floor to shut it, confirming that the door sealed appropriately. When had he last been in the fridge?

As he turned back towards his bedside, he froze, backing against the countertop when he saw a shadow lingering beside his bed. He watched it carefully for any sign of movement, seeing it extend an arm as though it was pointing at something. The fuzzy darkness seemed to engulf it, and it melted away slowly. He uttered his wife's name into the dark, slowly moving towards the kitchen table, where he noticed something small and golden and silver. It looked like a metal flower. He didn't recognize it.

As he reached for it, he heard the confident rap of knuckles against his front door. Once, twice, three times.

twenty-five

Lakin wondered if he was very quiet, would they go away? The visitor was likely Shaw, making sure that he hadn't fled town yet. Shaw probably wanted him to run so he could use that against him: a measure of guilt or an excuse to go after him. Would Shaw take it that far? At this point, Lakin didn't trust him at all.

The knocking repeated and Lakin knew that he'd never leave. If he didn't answer, Shaw would use his own key. He needed to take control of the situation with a little bit of confidence. He opened the door, keeping the edge against his shoulder so he could attempt to use his body to prevent any forced entry.

The person on the other side of the door, however, was not Shaw. It was Claire. The coldness of the night curled around him, sending a coarseness across his flesh. She did not seem bothered by the chill, standing quiet and motionless.

"Claire..." he said, realizing how groggy his voice sounded. "What are you doing here?"

"I need to talk to you about something, Mr. Douglas," she remarked matter-of-factly. "It's very important. Can I come inside?"

He remembered the last time Claire came into the cabin, how her demeanor had become subtly hostile. The way that she spoke with an edge and had a clear motive. He could see that same venom glimmering beneath the surface tonight.

"I guess I can't say no, right? It's your cabin," he said, trying to sound humored.

She raised a brow. "You can say no."

"That's not what I meant... I was just..."

It *was* what he meant, though, as she teetered there in the doorway like a vampire awaiting admission. She was just an extension of Shaw at this point, wasn't she? Maybe even a devious partner in crime, a mole, a spy. Or maybe she was also just a victim of his. He remembered her in the grocery store when they'd first met; she'd held some kind of kindness there. Or had he imagined so because that's what he wanted?

"Mr. Douglas?"

Lakin looked up at her, watching as she stood there expectantly. She offered him a small smile, "Are you okay?"

He opened the door wider without saying anything, and Claire entered, immediately discarding her jacket and hanging it on a coat hook that he'd never noticed. He didn't bother to sit at the table, hoping this conversation would be quick.

"What did you need to talk about, Mrs. Lowell?"

"Please, you know you can call me Claire."

He knew that, but he didn't want to. Just like she was calling him Mr. Douglas.

"So I know Shaw has asked you to stay in town... on account of Chitto's death."

Lakin nodded.

"First, I just want you to know that I know you didn't kill Chitto. I know you don't have anything to do with any of the things going on... I know. I think Shaw knows you didn't either, but he needs to blame you. Do you understand?"

"No," Lakin scoffed. "No, I don't understand. Why can't he face the fact that there's something else going on here? Something that needs to be addressed before it gets out of hand..."

Claire smiled at him, almost pitying. "He can't do that yet, but give him time. He will come to terms."

Lakin put a hand to his head; it was swimming with a stressed and tired delirium.

"I know you're afraid," she said, "You've been through a lot, and then you come here and there's all of this."

She took a step towards him and then another. Lakin didn't retreat, although he thought he wanted to.

"It'll all be over soon," she assured him.

"Are you afraid of him?" Lakin asked her quietly, acutely aware of the rapidly disappearing space between them.

"Who?" she asked, voice rising a pitch in curiosity.

"Shaw."

He felt silly suggesting it, even before she responded. If she was just wrapped up in this web of mayhem, she wasn't acting like she was worried or frightened. She was calm and collected. She stepped towards him again and he leaned away, but his feet betrayed him and stayed rooted. She brought with her an earthy, coniferous aroma. A dark, ripe, balsam fir. The odor of his church: the woods.

She laughed, and he could feel her warm breath on his face, "Why would I be afraid of him?"

Something about the way she said it made him uncomfortable, especially as she reached to run her fingertips up his chest and towards his throat before winding them into his hair. He tensed as they passed over his neck, seeming to apply the smallest amount of pressure there. Although the motion felt like a threat, like the suggestion that she could strangle him if she wanted to, he found himself leaning towards her now. The motion made him sick, stomach reeling like he had tipped over the edge of a cliff. The impact of their lips made his knees weak, and he stumbled towards her, pinning her body between his and the wall. Even as his mind told him he needed to stop and ask her to leave, something had him totally committed to reciprocating every motion she made.

Her hands traveled across his stomach and down to his pants, unsnapping the button and grasping the zipper. He grabbed her wrist, clutching it harder than he meant to. She looked up at him, eyes venomous. He was panting, he realized, and he struggled to catch his breath. He'd been a young boy once, thinking with everything except his brain. Somehow this was different; he felt like a passenger in a vehicle, body aching as he tried to stop this from escalating.

"We shouldn't... we shouldn't be doing this. You should really go," he forced himself to say.

He wasn't convincing. She didn't break eye contact with him, something humored flickering on her face.

"Or I can go," Lakin added.

She angled her chin up towards him, kissing him under his jaw. Lakin leaned into her, wrapping his arms around her waist as he lifted her up against him. He thought he heard her say, "You're not going anywhere." But he couldn't be sure.

He couldn't fight their movement to the bed, falling backwards onto the firm mattress so hard that his ears rang. She climbed on top of him and threw her shirt to the floor. A simple pair of black swallows were tattooed on her shoulder, looking like they were fluttering into the inky darkness as his vision became fuzzy and indistinct.

vi.

He ran out to her in his bare feet, screaming her name. He could see the glistening black gun in her hands.

His gun.

The one he kept in the closet and never used. He always took the rifle out when he was camping or on the river.

He didn't need that gun.

He didn't need it.

She didn't fight him when he reached down and wrenched the gun out of her cold hands, clutching it against his gut as he turned away from her, afraid the sight of her in such a state of misery might make him sick.

"I have this burden," she said, voice clear and calm. The only sign that anything was wrong was the stuffiness of her nose from crying and the hoarseness of her throat from the cold. "It's this heavy, suffocating thing. I feel like I carry this terrible darkness around and it hurts and I'm drowning... and nobody knows it but me."

twenty-six

He remembered remarkably little of the night before. At some point, he had fallen asleep and Claire had still been there. When he woke, she was gone and there was no real sign that she'd ever been there. He felt hungover, and he felt guilty. Not so much that he regretted what he had done, but he couldn't help but imagine how he would've felt knowing if Lena had cheated on him. Maybe everyone did it after a while. It certainly sounded like both Shaw and Claire slept around.

But he'd been robbed of all of the burdens of a tired marriage; an old marriage. At this point, he'd take back Lena to have to argue about either of them being unfaithful. To have been with her so long that he forgot what it was like before. To be annoyed at her nuances and all of her bad habits. These were struggles, not end-alls.

People were so weak when they sought comfort. Lakin had been looking for something since the day he'd lost Lena. It was why he'd returned to work so soon and, now, why he'd slept with Claire. It was a moment of weakness, the way she was driving the interaction with clear intent. She had a game plan when she came there that night.

She saw him.

That was all he needed to not turn her away. Anyone to convince him that he wasn't a ghost, that he wasn't some shell, ripped from spirit, like Lena had been. It hurt him now, more than it had since the day he lost her. The wound felt fresh, but he was thankful for that pain. It somehow offered him consolation, a reminder that he was alive. The numbness shattered, revealing what humanity he thought he'd lost.

He stumbled out of the bed and to the table where the metal flower sat, ready to take his mind off Claire by busying himself with the mysterious object. Who had left it, and when had they gotten into the cabin? While he slept? He grasped the small thing between his fingers, feeling the cool and sharp edges as he leaned to shine its curled petals in the early morning light. The rose-gold surface glinted, and as Lakin turned it over in his hand, he realized what it was.

He rushed over to the light switch, flipping it on to confirm the identity of the object. It couldn't be... but it was.

It was a smashed .30-06 round, and somehow he was sure that it was the one he had fired into the mysterious creature when it had killed Holly. Someone had found it and brought it here. He didn't know how they'd gotten the

cartridge, or how they'd broken into the cabin while he slept...
or, more importantly, why they would have put it here. He had
a creeping sensation that it was the creature, somehow. That it
wanted him to know. He had trouble imagining an animal who
possessed the mind of a man: capable of plotting and advanced
thought process, something both primitive and sentient.

His headache intensified and he dropped the smashed
cartridge onto the tabletop, letting it bounce and roll off to the
floor as he stumbled towards the refrigerator.

He wasn't surprised when the open door revealed so
little content. He reached for the half gallon of milk, swiping
away crust from the spout when he cracked the lid off before
turning up the entire carton like he was thirsting to death. He
hoped the liquid would both satiate his headache and offer him
some kind of fulfillment. He was so hungry. When had he last
eaten?

Lakin found himself dizzy, reeling at the thought of
food. He'd let his blood sugar get too low. He'd always been
able to go long periods between meals, but at this point it
might have been days since he had something. Maybe since he
met Chitto at the restaurant. He grabbed the corner of the
table as it collided with his thigh. He heard it creak beneath his
weight as he leaned into it. It scooted across the floor and he
lost his balance, falling all but face first onto the floor.

That shadow loomed again but seemed to recoil from the light of day. He thought he could see the front door creaking open, and four long and clawed fingers curled around the edge. Mismatched with the large hand, the smallest form of a child peered around the corner: a girl in a pink pajama set covered in blood and dirt, the door just barely hiding a mangled side of her face.

"It's okay, Mr. Douglas."

twenty-seven

Lakin was chilled to the bone. The instant he was awake and aware, he felt the convulsion of damp-cold ripple through him and he curled into himself. His entire body ached: from his shoulders to the soles of his feet. The stress was really getting to him; he had never passed out in his entire life... other than during the incident at the swamp.

The world swerved, pitched, and lurched around him when he finally opened his eyes. The expected ceiling of the cabin tore away into blue sky and the skeletal remains of distant trees. He was suddenly aware of the firm ground beneath him: clods of dirt and rock jabbing into his flesh. He sat up slowly, groaning with the effort and strain on his aching muscles.

More alarming than the fact that he was outside was the realization that he was naked.

And he was covered in blood.

He stood up, stumbling until he managed to make his way over to a rotting fence post, leaning against it heavily. It swayed in the muddy earth, threatening to give in to him entirely. The sun seemed brighter today than it had all winter. The season had been so dark, so without light. He tried to orient himself as to where he was, how he'd gotten here, and where his clothes were.

A woman's scream had him spinning around, seeing now that a pale Marie Baldwin and a young boy were standing in the space between him and their house.

"I told you, Ma," the boy whispered.

Had the boy found him out here while he was still asleep? Lakin suddenly clamped his hands over himself.

"Baby, go call Shaw right now," Marie whispered, not taking her eyes off of Lakin's face.

"No, no, no," Lakin pleaded, taking a step forward.

Marie put one hand out like she could stop him, using the other hand to shove her son towards the house.

"You stop right there, Mr. Douglas."

Tears brimmed around her eyes, lip quivering in fear. She did not falter, though, eyes opened so wide that they bulged, body rigid and unmoving.

"Marie... Please, calm down."

She screamed, "Mister... Douglas. Do not come any closer. The police are going to be on their way. Shaw will take care of this."

"This is just a misunderstanding."

"You're sick, Mr. Douglas. You need help. I should've seen it sooner. Just don't hurt me and my boys. It'll be alright, I promise. Just please don't come any closer."

"Marie, please!" Lakin repeated, voice rising. He took more steps towards her and she made a squeal in her throat.

"What are you doing here?" she whispered. "What have you done?"

"I—"

He didn't know what he was doing there, but until she had asked the question, he hadn't considered what he had done.

Lakin made a decision; he turned around and bolted across the field in the opposite direction. Marie didn't call after him, but he could hear her as she ran back to her house, screaming for the boys to lock the doors.

Lakin initially headed down the highway, but the fear of being seen fleeing in the nude had him cutting through the woods in the direction of the cabin. He would take the chance of encountering hunters or drug addicts; anything to avoid running into Shaw and his deputies or a station wagon carrying an innocent family into town.

The distance to the cabin couldn't have been far, unless he had miscalculated his route during his panicked delirium. He found himself skidding barefoot across a gravel drive and, at first, he grew concerned that he'd ended up at someone else's house... but he saw a sign that read: ROTTEN FORK FREEWILL BAPTIST CHURCH.

There were no cars in the parking lot, no obvious parsonage. He knew that churches were often unlocked, by principle. As much as he would normally be offended by the thought of stealing from an establishment like a church, he needed something to cover himself. There was likely a donation box of clothes, or someone's forgotten jacket, or even a sacred cloth. He'd take anything he could find right now.

The interior of the church was well illuminated, covered in pink and gold as sun filtered through the stained glass panes. He walked to the pulpit, now keeping his hands drawn around his chest, as though here it was more important to defend his heart than the rest of him. Behind a thin piece of plexiglass was a baptismal pool with water inside it. He thought perhaps someone had forgotten to drain it. Draped over the nearby chair was a white baptism gown, and it looked like it would fit.

He clambered into the pool, finding the water warmer than he had anticipated. That should have been his first indication that this was not simply water left over from a Wednesday-night baptism.

But Lakin hastily scrubbed away the crusted blood and dirt, turning the water the color of iron-tinged rivers. He pulled the plug loose from the drain, listening to the mesmerizing and consistent sound of the water rushing through the church's piping. It was interrupted by a sharp click that echoed around the sanctuary, causing Lakin to spin loudly around on his backside in the emptying tub.

In the aisle, a man in a suit stood just in front of a young man and woman. They timidly stood behind him: the man, more of a boy, was in a pale blue turtleneck. His pink-splotched face suggested a recently discharged youth, lips protruding slightly ahead of a pronounced overbite. The young woman at his side clung to his arm, doe-eyed and pink cheeked from the chill outside.

The man in the suit turned to the young couple, ushering them into a room just off to the side. When the light flipped on, Lakin noticed that the room was lined with books and contained a desk and a comfortable loveseat. While their backs were turned, he quickly slipped on the white gown, slick fabric clinging to his moist skin in the most immodest way. He twice had to pull it away from sticking between his legs.

"Good afternoon, sir." The man in the suit approached him in a relaxed way, as though everything was like it was supposed to be.

"I am so sorry," Lakin tried to explain. "I needed somewhere to wash off, and I have lost my clothes. I didn't know anyone was going to be here. I can return this..."

"Let me give you a ride, and you can keep the gown."

The man motioned for him to follow, and Lakin obediently tagged along to the little sedan parked outside.

It was comfortable, clean, and smelled like fake cherry. A small crucifix hung from the rear-view mirror, along with a sterling silver bobwhite quail charm. It was interesting how even this man of a religious faith still believed in some of the folk magic.

"Where can I take you?" the pastor asked, resting his hand on the headrest behind Lakin's head as he backed out of the parking lot.

"I'm staying in the Lowell cabin, just up the road."

In reality, Lakin didn't know how far he was from the cabin at this point. He should've been so close, and he'd always had good travel sense even without anything to show him direction... but he was so disoriented right now.

"Oh, you're the out-of-towner."

His voice hadn't changed from the soft tone. It didn't hold any kind of edge or suspicion. This kept Lakin at ease, but he could only nod his head and utter 'yep' in response.

"Is all well with your soul, Mr. Douglas?"

How did he answer that?

Nothing had been well with his soul since Lena had died. Before, if someone asked him to describe himself, there would have been a dozen hobbies, lifestyles, and adjectives he could have used to paint a picture of who he was. He might have mentioned he was a husband; he was sure it would've come up, but it wouldn't have been one of the first things he brought up. After she died, it was as though that was the only thing about him that mattered. Her absence somehow had more weight than her presence. She had ripped part of him away— all of the joyous and significant parts— when she left this world. Maybe she'd taken his soul with her. He wouldn't have been sure he had one when she was alive, but when she died... he suddenly had no doubt.

twenty-eight

Lakin shut the cabin door behind him and immediately changed into clean, comfortable clothes. The damp baptismal gown was abandoned in a silken heap on the floor. He retrieved his cell phone from the table where he'd left it. The battery was nearly dead, and he realized that he had been gone all day and night, and now into the next day.

Over twenty-four hours that he could not account for. His fingernails were broken and pulled away from their beds, and his fingertips were bruised. Had he fought off his attacker?

He had never updated his phone like he should have, and so it didn't have the battery life it once had. He plugged it into the charger and flipped through his notifications. He had five missed calls from Tyler and a text message that read: Hope everything is okay... worried that I can't get you. Call me asap. I'll be heading up tomorrow. Sent cleaned-up clip from security footage to your email. Hope it helps you out.

He almost didn't check his email, thinking that it could probably wait. He wanted to get out of this town, hire a good lawyer, and never step foot in Rotten Fork again... but he was also very curious.

He slung open the laptop so quickly that the hinges creaked. The fans whirred to life and he struggled with shaking fingers to type in his passcodes and log in for his email. Sure enough, the bold-black, unread email from Tyler sat at the top of the box, with a single attachment. He opened it, heart sinking as he struggled to comprehend what he was seeing on the screen.

The image was cleaned up surprisingly well: the darkest portions of the picture were grainy and full of noise, but the blue-green tone of night vision illuminated and smoothed out the bare skin of the woman on the screen. Her face was more visible now, and the bite wound on her shoulder was not a bite wound at all.

It was a pair of courting swallows inked on her skin.

The woman in the video wasn't Holly; it was Claire Lowell.

He was going to vomit. His head was swimming again, stomach sick and sour, and he was pouring sweat. He tried to reason it out and insist it didn't mean anything. That it didn't matter if it did mean something. He started throwing clothes into his bag, along with his computer and dying cell phone.

Then there was a knock at the cabin door, but Lakin didn't stop packing. The calm knock repeated and then he heard a voice from the other side. For a brief moment, he remembered seeing the child before he had passed out. He wasn't sure how he knew what Dulcie Lloyd looked like, but somehow he was confident that it had been her.

He walked slowly to the door, turning the knob carefully and opening it with great hesitation.

It was Claire, but it wasn't Claire. She seemed to lack some kind of luster and confidence. She looked sick. Her eyes were rimmed with pink lids and dark circles; her cheeks even seemed less full.

She didn't ask him if she could come in, but instead put her hand on his chest and pushed him inside as she entered, shutting the door quietly behind her.

"Where are you going?"

Lakin grabbed his bag and slid it across the floor to the doorway, ignoring her response.

"You can't leave."

He huffed, chest aching with stress. "You can't stop me, Claire."

"You don't understand... you can't leave."

He stopped, turning to look at her. He couldn't believe he was going to say this, and his tongue was paper-dry as he tried to speak, throat seizing with the lack of moisture. "Is it you?"

She nodded slowly, clapping her fingers gently against her palm.

"It was, yes."

Lakin rubbed his hand over his mouth, struggling to breathe. "You're the monster."

She shrugged one shoulder. "Subjective."

"Why the Lloyd girl? I get Tony... I even get Holly and Chitto. But why that little girl?"

Claire's lips curved into a soft smile, but he could not detect any remorse or pity there. It was like a mimicked expression that held no emotion, the cold reflection of a mirror. "That wasn't my fault. She got in the way... when I was out of control. I didn't want to hurt her. You believe me, don't you? I lost sleep over it. I can still see her face."

"Where is she now?"

"Gone. Long gone."

Lakin swallowed, backing away from her until he felt himself collide with the kitchen table. "Her parents deserve some closure."

Claire pursued, slowly. "I played with her like a doll all night. She was dead, already a corpse at that point. I was sick when I finally came to. You just... you get so intoxicated with the power. With the freedom, the wild. I used to fight it; I felt like I had to. But I've always been so emotional, and when you're feeling something a little too strong, it just breaks through. Shaw always cleaned up after me, once every couple of years. But I decided to just... let go, and then I couldn't stop."

"There's... no excuse for killing that baby."

"Oh, trust me, having that precious body's blood on my soul... I feel it every day. But that's my sin, not yours. That's between me and God. You don't understand what it's like, but you will."

"I... what?" Lakin's heart was pounding, and he felt like he couldn't breathe. His hands had a white-knuckled grip on the table behind him as realization began to sink in.

"Oh. Oh, you don't understand yet. You don't, do you? When I was just a little girl and we moved here, I was very sick. My parents hoped the country air would help improve my quality of life. It was terminal, you see. I didn't have a lot of time left. I didn't get out much and most of the kids just made fun of me. The only friend I had was Jae Boyd. It wanted her. Her dad was poking around in places he shouldn't; couldn't just leave things alone. Why can't we just accept that there are things we can't understand? Things we can't explain? He took me down there, and he gave me to it to save her. I was just a kid... but it cured me. Well, it put a hold on my disease. Shaw found out when we were just kids, and when you find something out like that, you can't just leave it be, you know? He loved me, and he promised to take care of me from that day on."

"Was that you at the Boyd place that day? You somehow made me think it was Simon Boyd? Have you been coming to the cabin at night?"

She smiled again but didn't respond to the questions. "I'm ready to just rest now, but I had to give this to someone else. Unfortunately it isn't that simple. You can't just give it to someone you know, someone familiar, someone who will tell and be believed. I needed you, Lakin."

"No," Lakin repeated. "No, no, no, no, no."

She leaned into him, hips resting against his, whispering a single word into his ear. Somehow, he couldn't grasp what it was. It was almost like a sound that wasn't human, that wasn't a word. He couldn't imitate or recognize it, and as soon as she'd said it he could no longer remember what it had sounded like... but it hit him like a physical force.

It collided with his soul, it pushed him out of himself. His skin was suddenly wet and cold, like a jacket you'd worn in the rain and couldn't wait to take off. His ears bellowed like they were filled with rushing air, and then everything started feeling distant and insignificant...

Just before he crashed back into his body.

twenty-nine

Something was happening to him.

It was a searing pain, like his body was on fire. He was screaming, involuntarily. He had never screamed like that before, and no pain he'd ever felt equated to what he was experiencing. Ironically, he thought he could smell burning flesh and hair: a smoky charcoal with the sulfuric, coppery undertone. He could taste it in his mouth, even through the overwhelming flavor of blood. His nose was bleeding, and he reached into his bloody mouth to feel teeth, sharp and pointed, erupting in front of his own. His head hurt, full of waves of pulsating pressure. Everything felt too tight, too small. He was nauseous, falling against the kitchen table as he struggled towards the bathroom. He found himself barking groans as he tried to vomit, voiding a bloody mess onto the table.

He didn't make it much farther, knees locking up and sending him planking flat onto the floor. He rolled onto his back, arching off of the floor as his back ached and tensed, contractions causing him to continue to froth and vomit through his mouth and nose. He tore off his shirt as sweat and tears poured down his face.

"Don't fight it," Claire said calmly.

He could hear popping and cracking that sounded like it was coming from inside him; the sound of someone fervently chewing hard candy. His head was starting to feel like it was full of cotton, pushing the softness out towards his ears and eyes and nose.

Lakin finally gave in. He wanted to die. He just let go and the relief was instantaneous. He was hot, his head felt too warm, but the pain had stopped. He felt like he was suspended, weightless. The cabin's quietness was deafening: the hum of the fridge he'd never noticed before, the drip of the faucet in the bathroom, and the soft breath from Claire's lips.

He looked at her then and realized he could also hear, or feel, the throb of the vein in her neck. A signal that she was becoming slowly more anxious, that increase of her heart rate in preparation for confrontation. In that moment, he realized he wasn't himself anymore. He was that thing, that monster, that beast. He was in control, but he wasn't in control. Thought and impulse were action; there was no consideration or latency between thought and response.

So when a furious rage overtook Lakin, he didn't have a chance to stop himself. He was lunging across the room on all fours, effortlessly knocking the kitchen table into the wall and smashing one of the delicate chairs. He wanted to ask her how she could have done this to him. He wanted to hurt her for the way she had hurt Holly and Chitto, but mostly for how she had hurt Dulcie.

Claire seemed to know he would come after her because she was one step ahead of him. She was out the front door and sprinting onto the highway in an instant. Lakin bolted after her, shoulders snagging against either side of the doorway, sending pieces of the frame bursting into the air with him.

He was clearing ground so quickly, and he was exhilarated with the thrill of it... until, suddenly, he was flooded with memories.

And they weren't his. They oozed through his subconscious in such a way that he could see clips like a slideshow on fast-forward. Despite this, they were sticky, residual. He could recall them perfectly, as though they were fresh. Vivid images of the lives of young women who had borne this: dozens of young Indigenous women, and the memories of one man who was so full of hate and fear that it had Lakin reeling. He saw Jae Boyd and the way that Simon Boyd had ripped the entity out of her young body so quickly that he had in turn destroyed her mind. Then there was Claire. He saw it all. Everything she had done and thought and felt as this creature.

He shook away the thoughts and memories, watching now as Claire headed straight down the center of the highway. In the distance he could hear the wail of a siren, and he thought he could even see the flash of lights appearing on the black pavement.

He headed after her again, closing the space that had grown between them. He saw the police SUV then, and it swerved to park crookedly in the road. Shaw stumbled out of the cab with a rifle in his hands, loading it with shaking hands. Lakin could smell his fear. He could taste the sour scent of sweat on the back of his tongue as he panted in the cool air. It excited him. He couldn't explain it. Was it finally having the upper hand on that douchebag? Was it that he might now get revenge for having been dragged through the mud by him?

Shaw's voice was shrill and panicked as he yelled Claire's name, his husky scream leaving a cloud of fog in the air above his head. She was sprinting as hard as she could to get away from Lakin, but he was slowing down. Something about Shaw's eyes, that terror of losing his wife, had him faltering. Hesitating despite his inability to think before. But that hesitation didn't last, because there was nothing else left to do. There were no choices to be made here, not for him. His hand was forced.

Shaw had a hold of Claire's arm now, dragging her not into the vehicle but beyond it. Lakin pounced onto the hood of the car, the shocks groaned underneath his weight, and when he stepped up onto the windshield, it cracked, leaving a spider-web pattern to spread across the surface. He clambered onto the top of the SUV and then peered down the back at Claire sitting on the pavement, looking up into his eyes.

"I'm sorry, Lakin," she whispered.

He heard a click, one that caused his body to jolt in surprise. He looked up as Shaw, standing only a few yards away, slid a silver cartridge into the rifle.

He raised the gun, he aimed, and he fired.

thirty

The wolf's body was gone, and now it was only Lakin's naked human body hanging over the top of the police vehicle. His chest heaved slowly, a terrible rattle echoing in his lungs before he stopped altogether. Claire got to her feet and went over to him, moving her hand across his face and through his dark and dense curls before letting his head fall to hang across the back glass again.

She walked to Shaw's side, and he collapsed onto the pavement, rifle clattering to the ground before he fell onto his knees. He was shaking, pale-faced.

"Claire..." he muttered, reaching over to grab her arm roughly. "Claire, what have you done?"

She did not jerk her elbow away, like she might have done in any other situation. Instead she smiled and put her hand on top of his, "What I had to do. Now we are free of this thing, of this place."

Shaw shook his head. "You'll die. You know that this was all that was keeping you alive."

She nodded slowly, and Shaw's eyes brimmed with tears. "Why would you do this to me? To us?"

"I did this for us," she insisted.

He started sobbing, "I don't know how to live without you, I don't want to figure out how."

"Well," she said. "You can cross that bridge when you come to it. Now, let's get this cleaned up... one more time."

She got to her feet and extended her hand to him, and Shaw hesitantly took it as he rose to his feet. He knew just the place, and no one would ever see Lakin Douglas again.

vii.

"I'm sorry, Lakin," she said.

He didn't turn around to look at her, wind biting at the tears that streamed down his cheeks. Why was she apologizing to him? He had failed her. He couldn't make her happy; he couldn't fix her. No matter what he did, she could not be cured. She still worried more about him, and how she affected him, than she did herself. He wanted more than anything for her to love herself, to see herself like he saw her: perfect, wholly pure.

"Lena, please. Please tell me what I can do... please tell me."

She didn't answer him, but instead she started wailing. She sobbed to God, she yowled incoherently like an animal in a trap: one that had all but torn off its trapped limb and found that even after chewing away its own flesh, the jaws of life would just not let go.

It had to let her go.

He had to let her go.

"I love you, Lena," Lakin said, turning around to face her. She looked up at him.

He raised the gun, he aimed, and he fired.

Epilogue

Tyler locked his doors, twice, on his way into Rotten Fork. Despite his love of the great outdoors and his aptitude for all things concerning nature and survival... he did not like rural America. He followed the GPS on his dash nervously, turning his truck down the desolate highway that would lead to the cabin where Lakin had been staying. Lakin hadn't reached out after Tyler had sent the video stills, and he thought it was the last straw... He couldn't wait any longer to make sure Lakin was okay.

He almost missed the short driveway to the cabin, noting that Lakin's vehicle was still parked out front. He breathed a sigh of relief and parked alongside it, making eye contact with an orange cat that had been sleeping on the hood. Tyler nodded at the cat awkwardly, and it laid its head back down, not bothering to look up even as Tyler exited the vehicle and headed towards the cabin.

The front door was ajar. The door facing was mangled. He saw brown fur stuck to the splintered surface, and he wondered if a bear had broken in to scavenge for food. In touristy areas, sometimes bears did that, especially when they were used to being fed... but this hardly seemed like a tourist trap, and Lakin wasn't stupid.

He didn't go inside the cabin. The moment he started to enter, he noticed the broken and scattered furniture, the puddle of blood on the floor. Lakin's bags were packed, but he was nowhere to be seen.

"Lakin? Jesus Christ..." Tyler found himself whispering before he raised his voice to yell. "Lakin!"

He hurried back to his truck, locking the door five times before he sent a text to his wife. She was no doubt still in her meeting and unable to respond to a call, but he had to tell her what he'd found at the cabin... and who he hadn't found. He pulled up a message from Lakin, scrolling until he found coordinates of the locust grove where he'd been doing his research.

Thank God, it wasn't far.

He peeled out of the drive, sending gravel flying onto the highway as he sped down the asphalt. He prayed that Lakin was there wading around in the mud without service on his phone. He'd kick his ass for this; he just wanted him to be okay. He wanted to bring him home.

He arrived at the old house that Lakin had messaged him about, and he put on his backpack and a mask, to protect himself from the fumes of the swamp, before he started across the field to the forest in the distance. As soon as he entered, he felt a great heaviness.

"Nope..." Tyler whispered to himself. "Nope... I do not like this..."

He stopped in his tracks, starting to walk backwards out of the trees, as though he was afraid to turn his back on whatever was there. Then he heard a voice from deeper in the forest.

"Hey, over here."

He paused, eyes scanning the rows and rows of grey and black trees. He couldn't see anyone, but the voice didn't sound very far away. Was it Lakin's voice? He couldn't tell.

"Lakin?" he asked. "Is that you?"

"Hey, over here," it repeated.

"Come on, man. Let's get out of here. There's some shit gone down at your cabin. We need to get you out of this town, now. We need to get us out of this town."

"Over here."

Tyler wavered on the spot, hair standing along his spine in warning.

He set his jaw and started back into the woods after the voice.